"I'm Brian Stone.

The warm moistness of his breath, as he bent closer to her ear in the noisy ballroom, sent a little shiver down Mandy's spine. "And who the devil are you?" he continued.

It seemed important to tell him, but noises roared in her ears, and for some reason, her pulse was racing. She leaned back so he could read her lips. "Mandy," she mouthed.

"Mandy," he repeated in her ear. "Amanda. That means—ah, yes, 'worthy of love.' Are you, Amanda?"

She missed a beat in their whirling travel, but he laughed and picked up the step again. "Amanda. How nice. You don't talk much, do you? In fact, you're the first girl I've danced with all evening who doesn't want me to feature her in one of my books. Cat got your tongue?"

EMMA GOLDRICK describes herself as a grandmother first and an author second. She was born and raised in Puerto Rico, where she met her husband, a career military man from Massachusetts. His postings took them all over the world, which often led to mishaps—such as the Christmas they arrived in Germany before their furniture. Emma uses the places she's been as backgrounds for her books, but just in case she runs short of settings, this prolific author and her husband are always making new travel plans.

Books by Emma Goldrick

Don't miss any of our special offers. Write to us at the following address for information on our newest releases.

Harlequin Reader Service
P.O. Box 1397, Buffalo, NY 14240
Canadian address: P.O. Box 603,
Fort Erie, Ont. L2A 5X3

EMMA GOLDRICK

silence speaks for love

Harlequin Books

TORONTO • NEW YORK • LONDON
AMSTERDAM • PARIS • SYDNEY • HAMBURG
STOCKHOLM • ATHENS • TOKYO • MILAN
MADRID • WARSAW • BUDAPEST • AUCKLAND

Harlequin Presents first edition June 1992
ISBN 0-373-11465-6

Original hardcover edition published in 1990
by Mills & Boon Limited

SILENCE SPEAKS FOR LOVE

CHAPTER ONE

SOMEONE had left a large wooden bar stool tucked in the corner of the ballroom, behind a screen of potted plants. Amanda Small leaned back against it, thankful for a chance to rest. Although it was a cool June night, she was perspiring. And for the first time that night she admitted to herself that it might work. She had already had four dances, and none of the men seemed either disappointed with her dancing, or over-curious.

To tell the truth, moving out on to the floor crowded with people had frightened her at first. Crowds had not been her thing since she had been returned to the United States alone, a forlorn fourteen years old. Her volunteer typing work for the Red Cross, her work as an aide at the paediatric clinic, all kept her in contact with people, but only in small groups. And there were hardly any men involved!

Sweet twenty-one, she chuckled to herself. And on my first dance date. For just a second she thought back in time, and almost regretted the years she had spent in the rose garden.

She smoothed down the bodice of her long blue dress. It fitted like a sheath over a full figure no woman need have been ashamed of. But it was her first ballroom dress, and she had to fight off the urge to pin it up, to cover the *décolletage* that displayed altogether too much of her unfettered breasts. Or did it? She had no answer. Her mother had died with her father in that terrible tragedy that had left Amanda an orphan. The dress

5

would have to do. She ran a hand through her cap of tight bronze curls, and twirled in her hidden corner.

There were two orchestras playing alternately at opposite ends of the huge 1890s ballroom. One band played rock and disco. The other was a polka band, which had just swung into a waltz, of all things. Mandy shook with silent laughter, her whole body quaking. Dancing lessons had been *de rigueur* for the only daughter of two medical doctors. She curtsied to the potted plant and extended her hand, only to find it trapped firmly in a large male palm!

While she was still considering, he swung her gracefully out of her corner and on to the dance-floor, without missing a beat of the music. She felt herself swept up in the song and the night, and picked up the rhythm quickly and surely. For the first few steps he held her at a distance, but as soon as he found her matching him he pulled her close, burying her head under his chin, her face pushed up against the soft brocade of his waistcoat.

Warm and cuddly, Mandy told herself. And so much bigger than me! She leaned back to get a good look at his face. Lean, like a hunter. Deep blue eyes, sandy hair, broad shoulders. He reminded her of—of her father, of course! Not in looks. He was nothing like her shaggy bear of a father—except for that aura of command which exuded from his every pore. He leaned down to speak to her, but the noise in the ballroom obliterated the words. He bent closer, his lips at her ear. The soft, warm moistness of his breath sent a little shiver down Mandy's spine. Is that what it means? her jittery mind demanded of her. Is he turning me on? Just like that? Wow!

'I'm Brian Stone, your host,' he said. 'And who the devil are you?'

It seemed important to tell him, but the noises roared in her ears, and for some reason her pulse was racing, her face flushed. She leaned back again so he could see her lips.

'Mandy,' she mouthed, over-exaggerating the pronunciation.

'Mandy?' he repeated in her ear. 'Amanda? That means—ah, yes, "worthy of love". Are you, Amanda?'

She missed a beat in their whirling travel, came down flatfooted, and shrugged her shoulders at him. He laughed, and picked up the step again. 'Amanda. How nice. You don't talk much, do you? In fact, you're the first girl I've danced with all evening who didn't want me to feature her in one of my books. Cat got your tongue?'

She laughed back at him, shook her head, and stuck out her tongue as evidence. The shake of her head activated her bronze curls and set them dancing, reflecting. The hairpin that held the roll at her forehead took that moment to desert, letting the bunched curls drop down over her face. He laughed at her discomfort. A tiny spurt of anger rose in her, and then dispersed, as he pulled her close again and ran a finger through the curls.

'Leave it, Mandy,' he said. 'It makes you look younger—different. Leave it that way.' His smile was comforting, and that in itself surprised her. She was famous for deep compassion, a happy-go-lucky attitude, and a monumental temper!

The music ended while she debated, but he twirled her around one more time before bringing her to a breathless halt. She still had both hands resting on his forearms, staring at him, when he bent over and kissed her lightly on the lips. She stood still, hands clasped behind her back now, savouring the bliss, her eyes closed. Nothing else happened. When she opened her eyes he was gone.

There was a moment of sorrow, but then her innate good cheer came to the fore. Dr Hinson's argument this morning, as he tried to talk her into coming to the dance with him, came back to her. 'Mandy, in spite of your problem, you've got more guts and common sense than any girl within a five-hundred-mile radius.' She laughed at herself again. Common sense, of course, she thought. There's not a very big market for that these days. But then, if Brian Stone is the host to this mad charity crowd, he must have a hundred girls that need rescuing here tonight. Go get yourself a drink and some fresh air, Amanda Small!

She wandered over to the trestle-top bar, picked up an already-poured paper cup of Coke, and handed over a five-dollar bill. The attendant smiled and returned one dollar. Mandy shook her head and grinned as she walked away, sipping at the flat drink. But it's all for charity, she consoled herself as she made her way out to the coolness of the veranda.

There were a few scattered wooden seats on the veranda. She walked to the end of the platform and settled down on one of them. The moon was dodging in and out of storm-clouds. Wearily she slipped out of her pumps and wiggled her toes. The garden stretched out in front of her, bigger by far than her rose garden, but almost uncared for. A profusion of bushes cut off large corners of it from the house, and weeds proliferated.

She smiled as she recognised within her the eternal nitpicking of an amateur gardener. And how about the night? So far, almost perfect. Her little gold wristwatch flashed eleven o'clock at her. There *was* one small problem. Dr Hinson, fifty, greying, had invited her to come with him. Insisted she come with him. Demanded that Amanda Small should not spend her twenty-first birthday at home, alone. Especially since his wife Betty was down with a sudden attack of the flu. And so he had bundled Mandy off—almost kidnapped her—to the town's first charity ball. He had danced with her once, and then had been called out on an emergency. All that more than an hour ago, and apparently he would not be back before the ball ended. Oh, well, she thought, looking disgustedly at her ballroom slippers, it's only two miles to home, and Cinderella can walk! With that minor problem set aside, she considered her major one. Him. Brian Stone!

She called back to mind every tiny bit of his appearance. She weighed every word he had said, knowing certainly that she could not forget a single syllable or pause. And then he had kissed her! The nerve of him! But she was smiling as she thought it all through.

It was hard to judge the effect of a kiss when you'd had so few. She sighed to herself. It had certainly not set off fireworks in her head. Her legs had not turned to jelly. But it had been nice. He smelled good, and he tasted good! There had been something of tenderness in it. All in all, a very satisfactory kiss! I must obviously be in love with the man, she teased herself, and laughed as she suppressed such a ridiculous thought. That sort of thing just didn't happen—not in Amanda's world. Still, she seemed to hear his warm, deep voice echoing in her ear.

It wasn't an echo; it was the real thing. He was down in the garden below her, smoking a cigar, and talking to some woman out of sight from Mandy's seat.

'It's a madhouse,' he said. 'An ever-loving madhouse. If I had known it would be like this I would never have given the committee permission to use the ballroom. Here were are out in the middle of the countryside, and we've got gatecrashers, teenage cuties, vandalism. Lord, I went upstairs to change my shirt, and there was a pair of them in my bed, if you can believe that. And somebody broke into the cellar and made off with ten bottles of Dom Perignon! Never again!'

'But it must have its compensations, darling,' the high, shrill voice insisted. 'We all saw you kiss that little redhead. Right in the middle of the dance-floor!'

'Nonsense, Maryanne,' he returned, laughing. 'A kid's joke. She couldn't have been more than sixteen. With her parents around some place, I suppose. And that wasn't red hair, it was bronze. A fine, natural bronze, soft as silk.'

'So you're a specialist now in women's hair?' The trill of laughter set Mandy's teeth on edge. It was jealous laughter.

'Hey,' he chuckled, 'a good writer has to know about all kinds of things. Besides, it's easy to tell a suicide blonde from the real thing.'

The remark must have hit on some sensitive spot. The woman said very coldly, 'Just what do you mean by that?'

'What? Suicide blonde?' he asked. 'It's an old joke. A suicide blonde is one who dyed by her own hand. Funny?'

It apparently wasn't. The woman muttered an incoherent something and stalked away. He chuckled again, took one more puff on his cigar, then flipped it out into the garden and walked away.

Well! Mandy grinned at her own reaction. So what did you expect? she asked herself. Instant love? Mount my steed, beauty, and we'll ride off into the sunset together? So he had been subtly sharp with the blonde, and more than a little abrasive. Although Mandy grinned, there was a little—just a tiny—feeling of pique. Just a kid! Perhaps she should have brought the letter with her and pinned it on her—bosom? The letter, of course, had been a terrible start to this wonderful day.

She had slept late, after spending a long night in St Anne's Hospital, comforting a fourteen-year-old girl who thought that her scars would bring an end to her world. Until she saw how Mandy handled her *own* problems. So when Mandy woke up, Mrs Purcell had left a letter on the hall table, and a long note about resigning her position.

Barton, Brown and Burns. The name on the envelope was enough to upset her. One of them had been her legal guardian for seven years. She had never been sure which. How could you have a legal corporation for a guardian? They managed her funds, paid her bills intermittently, kept her staffed with a housekeeper, and once a year sent her a birthday card, along with a statement of her assets. Only this morning it had been a little different.

'We congratulate you on the occasion of your twenty-first birthday,' the letter said. 'Since you are now legally of age, our guardianship ceases as of this date. We will, should you instruct, be honoured to continue the management of your funds at our usual fee!' Happy birthday, Barton. Or Brown. Or Burns! She had shown it to Dr Hinson when she went in to his free orthopaedic clinic to do her volunteer secretarial work. And he had immediately checked with his wife, and then insisted on taking her to the ball!

The band in the ballroom behind her crashed into a serving of hard rock, and Mandy had lost her zest for that. She got up slowly from the bench, stretched, and sauntered to the stairs that led down into the garden. It would have to be a quick look, she decided. The moon was losing its war with the storm-clouds, and June rains on Thackery Point were generally drenchers. But her head was aching, and she had a need to go. She hiked up her tight skirts to keep them clear of the clutter, and started down the winding path that led into the gloom of the trees.

There had once been an extensive bed of tulips, she could vaguely see—all gone now, with their stalks almost buried under an attack of weeds and wild dandelions. She paused at a turn where moonlight lit an old, tired rambler, festooning an equally old and tired trellis. She stopped to sniff at one of the large blooms. Its scent was hardly noticeable among the last of the overpowering lilacs. There was an iron bench just ahead, spotlighted by a shaft of moonlight. It welcomed her quietly. Her feet were really beginning to smart. Her choice of shoes had been a total disaster.

She sat gracefully, pulled off her pumps again, and wiggled her toes. The slight rising wind ran through the trees around her with a sigh. She leaned back against the bench, squirming to be comfortable against the wrought-iron back, and let the wind play across her face and toy with her hair. It was a time and a place for re-membrance, and she remembered. She had been evacu-ated to Massachusetts Children's Hospital, and it had been there, four days later, that the social worker had told her she was an orphan.

Her own psychiatric treatments had held her in the hospital for two months, and then she had been released and sent home. Sent home! Even now the thought chilled her. How could it be home, without her father and mother there? She had been sent home to an empty house, and the judicious care of Barton, Brown, and Burns, the law-firm which had been appointed her guardian. And whose only real effort had been to hire Mrs Amy Purcell. Mrs Purcell, a bitter, gaunt widow, who believed that physical affliction was a punishment straight from God. And who had ruled the little lost girl with equal amounts of stern discipline, frequent complaints, much prayer, and no love at all.

Mandy, in order to survive in this loveless world, had developed an iron will, a strong sense of independence, and had built herself a narrow little world entirely her own! It was only in the last year that she had been free from that horrible dream.

Mandy shook herself out of her wanderings. The breeze was stronger, and chilly. Time to get up and go home, girl, she told herself. Her headache seemed to be growing stronger. She stood and stretched, flexing the stiff muscles in her shoulders. It was then that she heard the voices coming down the path. Three men, coming around the curve towards her, laughing at each other's jokes, each waving an open bottle in hand. Not men, really. Boys. Seventeen? Well-dressed, and drunk. The moon came out at just the wrong moment, highlighting her dress.

'Hey, what have we got here?' one of them shouted. 'All alone, babe? Want some company?'

Mandy drew back against the bench, out of the circle of moonlight. They were only children, but dangerous in their newly matured strength. Talk them out of it, the pamphlets all said. Be polite, but firm. Nice in a pamphlet, but hard to do on a dark garden path, and Mandy

knew her limitations. She had realised them when she
was fifteen, and had taken up martial-arts instruction.

It had not been her own idea. She had gone back to
school almost a year after the accident, and in one day
the word had spread. That afternoon, when she had
come out of the building, a group of freshman boys had
ringed her on the stairs, chanting, 'Dummy! Dummy!
Dummy!' She had tried to break away from them, but
they had kept throwing her back into the centre of the
circle.

At that point Ralph Dumbrowski had come out. He
had been her neighbour for years, and a co-captain of
the basketball team. In one mad rush he had knocked
down one of the boys and thrown two more over the
edge of the stone stairs into the rose-bushes. And that
had ended Mandy's problems for the rest of her school
years. It had been Ralph who said, while comforting
her, 'I might not always be here, Mandy. You'd better
study karate.' And so she had.

'What's a doll like you doing out here?' her tor-
mentor repeated. One of them swung around her in a
wide arc to get on her other side. She trembled, but con-
trolled herself. Which probably triggered the next event.
Just a few words, a joke, anything, might have sent them
on their way, but that was beyond Mandy's ability. So
instead of passing her by they closed in, arms grabbing.

It was a slow-motion operation, as if they were stalking
a rabbit. For a second her mind panicked, and she
screamed a terrible voiceless scream. But her iron will
regained control. She lifted both hands in a parrying
motion, and turned sideways towards the nearest one as
he lunged at her. She grabbed his outstretched arm, fell
down and away from him, and used his own weight and
momentum to throw him gracefully over her hip. He

smashed head-on against his friend on the other side. The pair of them thrashed around in the bushes, cursing, while Mandy bounded to her feet.

The third boy decided that it must have been a lucky accident. He came at her with both hands up, boxer-style. There was just enough moonlight for her to see his right hand coming at her in a wild roundhouse curve. She stepped forwards, inside the swinging arm, and jolted him in the solar plexus with stiff fingers, then chopped down on his throat with the hard edges of her palm. He staggered back a pace or two, clutching at his stomach, sat down abruptly, and began crying.

The tears so startled Mandy that she forgot the other two, who had by now managed to regain their feet. They came at her from behind. Two pairs of hands seized her shoulders, ripping the soft material of her sleeve. The dress tore away as she jumped forwards, ripping down the right side, and stripping her to the waist.

'Look at that,' one of them mumbled. 'Grab her. We'll show the little bitch a good time!'

Mandy gave up trying to restore her dress. Her blood was up, the blood of a long line of Smalls that led all the way back to the docks of Bristol town. She moved to one side, so that her assailants were coming at her one behind the other. The leader was wary, but driven. Mandy sighed, and went into her programme. It was a routine she had practised often on dummies, but never for real. She shrugged her shoulders, hiked up her long skirts until her knees were free, all the time smiling at her would-be assailant. He evidently mistook her smile for an invitation, a coming of Christmas in June. He closed in on her, arms outstretched, and pulled her hard up against his body. Which was, of course, exactly where she wanted to be.

'Now——' he yelled in her ear. Whatever the rest of his message was she cared not a damn. Now it was! She shifted all her weight to her left foot and brought her right knee up into his groin with all the force she could muster. He took one staggering step backwards, a look of disbelief on his face, and then began screaming as he doubled over in pain. His screams mounted in pitch and strength as he coiled up on the ground, his legs kicking. From the distance someone else was thrashing around through the bushes, and a deep male voice yelled, 'What's the matter?'

Her third assailant heard it too. He bent over to help his still screaming friend. The crying boy had long since disappeared. The injured man seemed unable to walk. Mandy shrugged her shoulders. She could see no reason why she should offer to help either of them. Behind her she could hear running feet thudding down the path. The two boys, arm in arm, staggered around in circles, the screams dropping off to soft whimpers. They found the path, and made off slowly.

It had been a startling experience, beginning and ending in barely three minutes. And now her control slipped. She sank back on to the welcome support of the bench. Breathing was hard, her nerves were shaken, and her mind grappled only vaguely with the sequence of events. Come on, now, she chided herself as she bit at her lip. Get a grip on yourself!

The standard instruction was to first control your breathing. She tried it, breathing in deeply, holding for a count or two, and then exhaling. It worked. Just as all her practised but untested defence tactics had done. She relaxed against the back of the bench, and a timid smile flashed across her lovely face. I did it! I did it! Her mind busily congratulated her, while her eyes searched through the fading moonlight for her clutch bag. She staggered to her feet and wiped the perspiration from her forehead.

The bag had fallen under the bench in an awkward position. She stared at it, arms akimbo, legs astride. Yeah, lucky Amanda, she told herself. The torn side of her dress flapped in the rising breeze. Oh, well, she thought, there's no other way. She dropped down on hands and knees to worm her way under the bench. One hand brushed aside the compost of accumulated leaves. And that was the moment when Brian Stone came around the curve of the path at full speed, barely in time to see her assailants struggling off in the darkness. He took a few steps in their direction, then turned back. Mandy squirmed backwards out from under the bench. He grabbed her around the waist and hauled her to her feet.

'So it's you,' he muttered. And then in a louder voice, 'What are you, some sort of congenital idiot? You came down here as far from the house as you can get, with a pair of tough kids like those. You ought to have your head examined. You're a damn lucky girl that I happened along when I did, let me tell you!'

Mandy gaped at him in astonishment. He was at her side so suddenly that her right arm was already drawn back to chop at his throat, before she recognised who he was. Her mind sent out a recognition signal to all her nerves, and her entire body seemed to collapse. Luckily his arms were close enough to do for her what her legs would not; he pulled her back up from her slouch and cradled her against his chest.

Not until then did her mind get back in gear, fighting through the pains of the increasing headache. I'm a damn lucky girl! It seemed to her now that she had handled everything most satisfactorily. In fact, the war had been over before he appeared on the scene. I really deserve some kind of medal, she told herself. After all, it happened on his property, and therefore they were *his* thugs! But how can you tell that to an arrogant male, who obviously sees himself in the White Knight role?

And then for a moment she remembered her mother, as they sat in the kitchen shelling peas. 'Yes, I always do what your father tells me,' her mother had said. 'And when he's angry I always agree with whatever he says. Always.'

And Mandy, a suspicious seven years old, had said, 'Always?'

'Always,' her mother had returned. 'Oh, yes. That's the only way to handle a man!' So why had Mother laughed so hard right after she'd said that? Laughed so hard that she almost fell off the kitchen stool? And now here, why was this man—so angry?

She knew why he was staring at her. Her dress was torn halfway down one side, and she had purposely not worn a bra, because of the deep *décolletage* of the dress. As a result, he was getting a most attractive free show! She snatched at the tag ends of the gown, pulling it up to provide a minimum cover.

'What's the matter?' he growled. 'Did your boy-friends get a little too amorous for you? Are you all right?'

She nodded her head to the third question, and reached out her free hand in a gesture of appeal. 'Oh, all right,' he muttered. 'Let's get back to the house and see if we can reconstitute your dress!' He took her hand in his and began to tug her up the path. She stumbled, unable to keep his pace with her much shorter legs. And then she remembered her shoes. She pulled at his hand and managed to break free. He stopped while she went back, picked up her pumps, and rejoined him.

'Now?' he asked sarcastically. She nodded her head, and they started up the path again. There were tears in her eyes, and she was a girl who never cried. She would never have cried over her assailants, but now the danger was past, and *he* was angry with her. Furiously angry, and she couldn't understand why. No more than she could understand herself. Why in the world would she want Brian Stone's good opinion? Here he was, leading her back up to the house, acting like an angry bear!

He took her into the house by a side door, avoiding the ballroom completely. She had stemmed her tears by that time, but he could see the line they had made through the light dusting of powder she wore. She smiled tentatively at him, a warm, timid smile. His face was stern.

'For heaven's sake, child,' he grumbled, 'cover yourself up. This is no strip-joint that I'm running!' His hand reached down for the errant flap of her gown and drew it up against her shoulder. She snatched it away from him. As her hand touched his she felt a spark of massive emotional impact flash between them. It was something she had never felt before. Never *dreamed* of feeling. But it seemed to have no effect on him. His face remained impassive. She sniffed at a recalcitrant tear. He slowly shook his head from side to side.

'I'll never understand why I agreed to this damn ball in my house,' he snapped. 'I'm overwhelmed by drunks, pot smokers, and now this. Why the hell couldn't you wait until you got out of here? Or take them out in the back of your car? Lord help me, when I danced with you I would have sworn you weren't that sort of girl!' He was holding her up with both hands, looking at her as if she were some specimen of field-mouse he had just found in his kitchen.

'Oh, hell!' he snapped. 'Down here.' He pushed her down the hall, opened the last door on the left, and almost threw her into a quiet, semi-dark room. The flames in a fireplace gave the only light. It was some sort of study or library. 'Sit down there,' he directed. 'I'll get Mrs Duggan to come along with a needle and thread. We'll see that you're decent enough to get home. And look, little girl—the next time you get in trouble, try screaming earlier. They could have raped you if I hadn't gotten there when I did!' The door slammed behind him.

Reaction set in. She staggered to the nearest chair and fell into it. Her shoulders were bruised, and the muscles in her side ached where she had so suddenly called on them to throw her first opponent. Her head ached so terribly. She touched a palm to her forehead. It burned at fever pitch. Her eyes still close to tears, she hugged herself tightly and drew her feet up into the chair. What a mess! What an inglorious mess. It had all seemed so good, and then in a matter of minutes the whole world had tumbled in on her.

Her eyes wandered around the room. A clock, ticking over the fireplace, said a quarter after twelve. No wonder, she thought wryly. My carriage has turned into a pumpkin, and Prince Charming has turned out to be as big a bully as all the rest of them!

When the door opened she jumped, unable to contain her anxieties. This time the intruder was an elderly woman bearing needle and thread. She clucked as she examined the damage.

'Poor child,' she comforted. 'Wipe those eyes now.' She handed over a huge handkerchief. 'And the dress?

Ah, that's really only a little damage. Stand up, child, while I stitch that back in place.'

Mandy found herself following directions automatically. A few tucks, a quick flash of the needle, and the gown was restored. 'At least well enough to get you home,' Mrs Duggan said. 'Now, child, sit you down here for a minute. Just because you had a fight with your feller, it doesn't mean the end of the world.' She walked across the room and poured something from a decanter into a brandy glass. 'Drink a sip of this,' she continued, 'and then you can go back to the ball. And you call me if you need any more help.'

Mandy looked at the glass suspiciously. One day when she was sixteen she had stolen a dram from Mrs Purcell's bottle. Once, just on a dare with herself. She had almost choked to death on it, and the reprimands had lasted for weeks. But this drink went down easily, warming her chilled insides. She moved over to the fire and dropped gracefully to the hearth in front of it. Mrs Duggan watched her for a moment, then remembered urgent duties in the kitchen, and slipped away.

CHAPTER TWO

THE flames were hypnotic. She stared into them, reflecting. Brian Stone. He owns this house. He's a writer. He has a girlfriend—maybe more than one, I guess. He thinks that I'm a flaming fool, a congenital idiot, not yet out of nappies. And me? Why is any of that important to me? I've lived all my life in Thackery Point without ever meeting him before, and I'll probably never ever see him again. Maybe I should go home and write him a long letter about how much I admire him, and sign it 'anonymous'. She was beginning to recover her usual sense of humour. What had happened had happened, and was over. Now if only this crazy headache, this aching in her bones, would all go away!

She could still hear one of the bands playing, but the attraction was gone. She huddled closer to the fire, putting her hands out to be warmed. The quiet swarmed around her, absorbed her, until suddenly she realised that it was *too* quiet. The band had stopped playing some minutes before. There had been a bustle in the hall, and now even that was gone.

Come on, Mandy, she told herself. Cinderella had stayed a minute past midnight, the ball had turned out to be a colossal flop, and it was time to get back to the rose garden. She flowed to her feet with the graceful poise of a dancer, walked quietly to the door, and opened it. Two couples were standing at the door of the improvised cloakroom. She queued up behind them, and was restored to her lovely handknitted shawl. Amanda Small, she whispered to herself, lots of people love you, even though none of them is here tonight!

Refreshed in mind, she followed the last couple to the door. Everyone else had gone. She tossed her shawl over her shoulders and squared her chin for battle. She was the last, and her host still stood at the door.

He touched her with a warm hand, holding her arms perhaps a little longer than necessary. His brow furrowed. Oh, lord, Mandy thought, let him please remember who I am. Let him at least remember!

'So, Amanda,' he said. She smiled at him, a broad, warm smile. She nodded. 'And have you recovered from all that nonsense?' he asked. She smiled, and nodded again. 'Well, it was good to meet you,' he said softly. 'You're a brave child.' And he bent over to kiss her lightly. 'Goodnight, Mandy, whoever you are.'

The door closed behind her before she came back down to earth. She rubbed her hand gently over her mouth, cherishing his touch. A wild feeling of exultation ran up and down her back, a fierce feeling of triumph. She could feel tears running down her face, even though she was not crying. She looked around in dismay. She was standing under the roof of a small entry-porch, and the sky was spitting at her.

Water. Lord, how she hated having it come down on her head. It was all part of the African dream. She stepped out from under the roof and looked over the large paved area to her right. It was empty. Her memory recalled that Dr Hinson had been called away. He and his elderly Buick had disappeared on an emergency call, and had not come back. The outside lights began to click off, one after another, leaving her alone in the dark. Another splatter of rain struck in her face.

I'll just have to walk, she sighed to herself. And quickly! She pulled her shawl up over her head and stepped out down the drive, hardly making six paces when her feet began to file complaints about her shoes. Ten paces more, and the rains came. Not in dribbles, but in sheets, slanting down at her under the strength of a cold, whipping wind. She was soaked in seconds, wet right through. It was becoming harder for her to hold on to the present. The thunder rolled overhead. She ducked her head. Like the rolling barrage of the mortars, it sounded. Unconscious of what she was doing, she bit her lip.

Two more steps and her cup ran over. Her heel caught in a pot-hole in the drive. She slipped on the wet surface and stumbled into the thorny hedges that shaped the arc of the driveway. Mandy struggled up, managing to impale herself more than once on the thorns. And then the size of her catastrophe hit. She was soaked, aching, bleeding, alone, discouraged, and more than two miles from home. She took another straggling step towards home before her ankle became a mass of pain. It was too much for even the most sensible of girls. The rose garden was just too far away. Mrs Purcell had gone home to her sister in Newport. And the rain came down, this time augmented by tears—buckets of tears.

She turned around and struggled back to the shelter of the little porch. There was a bell button in the middle of the door. She pushed it with all her strength, then leaned against one of the wooden pillars holding up the roof. She was shaking now, from the cold chill of the rain, and perhaps something else. No answer. She pushed the button again, then banged on the door with her raw fists, and still no answer. She banged again, futilely, in the middle of the cacophony of the storm. Determination turned to despair. Weary beyond thinking, she slowly lowered herself to the soaked wooden floor of the porch, and wrapped her arms around the base of the pillar. I'm determined not to cry any more, she told herself firmly. Crying never helped! Crying was for little things, by little people. One never cried at a major catastrophe. She cuddled her head against the pillar, feeling the water cascading over her. Welcome to the real world, Amanda Small, she told herself. Happy birthday!

She could hear the clock striking in the tower at the Town Hall, nearly a mile away. Two heavy strokes. It was the sound that sent her over the edge, the terrible sound of the bell tolling. Amanda Small crumpled into the corner, coiled herself up in the foetal position, and shivered in terror as the terrible black door in her mind swung open. There were memories hiding behind it, yet, strangely, after the memories had run their course she was so stricken with terror that she commanded herself to forget. And so the door would close, and Amanda would never recall what happened. Until next it opened. And the only sign of its existence was the terrible grip it maintained on her vocal cords. And now the memories flowed.

They were all at the medical mission at Utangi, up on the knoll above the Serengeti plain. Her father and mother, both doctors, volunteered to serve for one year in support of the Peace Corps medical station. The rebels appeared at two o'clock in the afternoon, coming up out of the rain preceded by their mortar attack. An undisciplined mob, they were fleeing from defeat at the hands of the government troops. They smashed their way past the station's feeble defences, and set about putting every living thing to the sword.

'Don't make a sound,' Amanda's mother whispered as she hid with her young daughter in the hall cupboard. 'Don't make a sound or they'll kill us all!'

A small request. Don't make a sound or they'll kill us all. But fear was so strong that the child could taste it. As heavy feet thudded down the hall she whimpered. Her mother had thrown her own body over the girl's when the door was thrown open and the machine-gun rattled. Squashed in the dark, totally destroyed by fear, Amanda Small felt the dripping of liquid down across her forehead.

The massacre ended by three o'clock. The rebels took all the bodies, living and dead, out into the tropical rain and threw them into the lake. The government troops arrived at four. Two hours later they found the girl, the only living thing atop Utangi. Fourteen-year-old Amanda Small remembered that little whimper and her terrible guilt, and then blessedly forgot it all as the dream faded.

And now it was two o'clock in the morning, in faraway Massachusetts. Two o'clock, and the rain was beginning to let up. There was a noise behind her, a rattle of chains and the click of a latch. She managed to look over her shoulder. The front door was swinging wide and she could see, silhouetted against the lights inside, a man and two huge dogs. The dogs sensed her immediately. While the man struggled to close the door, the dogs strained at their leashes, growling.

'Liza! Mitchell!' the man roared. 'Sit. I can't get this damn door closed.' The dogs obeyed instantly, but sat at the ends of their chains. Their two heavy heads wove back and forth not more than three feet from Mandy's frightened face. She shrank back against the pillar, trying to condense herself into invisibility. Brian Stone turned

from the door and saw her, huddled up in a little ball,
with only the white of her shawl in view.

'What the hell?' he snapped. 'Guard!' He dropped
both the leashes and both dogs moved closer. The smaller
of the two opened her huge mouth and gently seized
Mandy's upper arm. She was too frightened to move.
Meanwhile the man had stepped back into the house and
snapped on the porch lights. When he came out again
she could hear him mumble under his breath, but his
voice seemed far away, and hollow.

She felt the relief when the dog dropped her arm on
command. She could feel the warmth as his arms swept
her up. She could feel the rainwater cascading off her,
and all over his dry clothes. She could feel the warm
comfort of him as he carried her down the hall and into
the study.

'Mrs Duggan!' he yelled, and then immediately, 'Oh,
hell, she's gone home already!'

He shifted Mandy's weight slightly in his arms, and
lowered her on to the hearthrug before the fire. He was
back in a few hazy minutes, his arms filled with towels
and blankets.

'Easy now,' he comforted her. 'Wrap this around you.'
He did all the work. Mandy was in a complete daze,
unable to control her shaking body, her eyes filled with
unshed tears, her head aching intolerably. Why fool
around with crying? she asked herself. But the daze was
too much for her, and she cried anyway.

'We've got to get you out of those wet clothes,' he
barked as she struggled against him feebly. It made sense
to Mandy, in a wild, crazy sort of way. She made no
objection as he slipped her out of her soaked dress,
stripped off her tights and briefs, and began to towel
her down vigorously. He worked hard at it, starting at

her feet and working his way upwards gently, until
warmth returned to her.

When he came to her heaving full breasts he stopped,
muttered something under his breath, and then went on.
As soon as he finished with her shoulders he wrapped
a blanket around her before making an assault on her
hair. He pulled her into a sitting position, kneeling
behind her as his busy hands worked. The warmth was
beginning to relax her. She leaned against him, feeling
his strength at her back, and hardly noticing that the
blanket had slipped down into her lap.

'For—cover yourself up, child!' he snapped.
'Whatever made me think you were a child?'

She was still in the grip of terror, but her hands reluctantly retrieved the blanket. Her mind seemed open
to invasions of fantasies. He stood up, and seemed to
grow and grow until his head was almost lost in the
beams of the ceiling. He can't be that big, she told herself
in her delirium. He can't be! The whole room seemed
to waver.

'Does that make it a little better?'

She nodded.

'I have to let your people know where you are,' he
said. 'What's your telephone number?'

She looked at him blankly, then wormed one of her
long, thin hands out from under the blankets and made
a writing gesture. He was puzzled, but his attention was
distracted by the blood still oozing down her arm. He
picked up a pad and pencil from the desk and dropped
it beside her. 'Write it down,' he ordered, 'while I get
something for that arm.'

She watched him through her haze as he went to the
door. Then she freed her other arm and quickly scribbled
her telephone number on the pad. She was thoroughly

wrapped up when he appeared again, with only her bleeding arm in view. He brought a basin of water with him, and a variety of health aids. His gentle fingers bathed her arm, freeing it from the encrusted dirt and dried blood. When he switched to the antiseptic she hissed in pain. He drew back and waited for her to say something, but she remained silent.

He applied a pressure bandage, then picked up the pad where she had written her number. 'I'll call your home first,' he said, 'and then the doctor. I don't like the look of that arm, and I think you've started a fever.'

He was gone for another ten minutes, according to the pendulum clock on the mantel. Mandy managed to wrap herself up completely, throwing one of the towels over her head to make a hood. Her teeth were chattering. She moved closer to the fire, still in a troubled daze. When he came back there was a frown on his face, and he had her bag in his hands.

'Nobody answers at your house,' he said. 'I rang three times. The doctor will be along as soon as he gets through with the three-car accident on Route 88. So I can't get you treated, and I can't take you home. What shall I do with you?'

She looked up at him with an appealing motion of head and shoulders. He studied her. 'Then we'll just have to put you up for the night,' he concluded. She nodded.

He stood up and walked around her, staring at her curiously. She felt threatened, and drew back from him, almost into the fire.

'Am I deceiving myself?' he asked. 'If it weren't for the fact that you told me your name on the dance-floor— and you screamed down in the garden—I would have sworn that you've not made another sound all night. Not a sound! What the hell's going on, Amanda?'

She shuddered. Her hands crept out from beneath the blanket, which immediately slipped to her lap. She held out her arms towards him in silent appeal. Her fingers waved in strange patterns. 'Come on,' he snapped, 'it's three o'clock in the morning, and I'm in no mood for parlour games. Speak up!'

Her mind was too cluttered to respond. She stood up gracefully, letting the blanket slip to the floor. He gasped as she stood nude before him, silhouetted against the flames. She took the one step necessary to reach her bag, opened it, and extracted her little metal 'Medic-Alert' tag. She handed it to him and watched his mobile face as he scanned the message embossed on the tag. The light bothered him. He moved closer to the fireplace. She knew the message by heart. It listed an emergency telephone number across the arc of the top. Then, under it, it said, 'Patient is mute. Mild hydrophobia.'

'Oh, my aching back,' she heard him mutter in the distance, even though he was moving towards her. Her mind was wrenched back for just an instant into the past. She whimpered, and her mother whispered in her ear, 'Don't make a sound, or they'll kill us.' It was the last sound Amanda Small had ever made. Brian Stone was just in time to catch her as she gave up the struggle and drifted into unconsciousness.

CHAPTER THREE

BY THE time the sun straggled up over the Atlantic there were still wisps of low-riding clouds, black with rain, rushing north-east. Some birds had returned to life, but the main sound was the raucous call of the seagulls as they rose from sheltered waters, and from the massive flat roof of the shopping malls in Dartmouth. Mandy heard nothing of this. The excitement of the night before and the thorough soaking had been too much for her. By eight o'clock in the morning her temperature had risen to one hundred and five degrees, and she was having difficulty breathing. She tossed and turned on the great bed, but knew nothing.

In spurts of consciousness during the next few days she heard voices come and go. She felt tender hands touch and probe her. She felt cool water, and a change of clothes. And along with these sensations she knew the constant presence of a massively strange head, resting on the edge of the bed beside her. It breathed heavily, and from time to time it yawned, displaying a cavern full of monstrous teeth. The head, the noises, and the touching, these were all she knew.

In fits of lucidity she tried to fill in the blanks. Somewhere in her mind the phrase kept ringing, 'I love him.' I love whom? The head with all those teeth? Or a shadow that she remembered, towering over her, brooding, stretching all the way up to the ceiling? Another figment of her imagination? Who in the world would love Amanda Small? Her head ached excruciatingly, as if twenty devils were beating on her with hammers. She had trouble breathing again, and panic seized her. The outside lights were suddenly shut off, and she lay quietly in a grey world, listening to the soft hissing of oxygen as it was pumped into the plastic tent that surrounded her. She drifted into a sleep of forgetfulness, hardly noticing the needles that pierced her arm. And then, just as suddenly as everything else that had happened to her, she woke up to sunlight, rested, weak, and curious.

The head was still there. A dog. One of the two who had guarded her at the door during that deluge—last night? It rested there, unblinking eyes on her face, until it saw her move. A great tongue swept out at her, caressed her hand. Its tail wagged a welcome, beating noisily on the hardwood floor. The noise awakened Mrs Duggan. She had been napping in the rocking-chair by the window.

'Well, and you've come back to us,' the housekeeper said cheerfully. She got up slowly and walked over to the bed, rubbing her side. 'Sitting all hours leaves me stiff,' she said chuckling. 'Drink some of this.' She held a cool glass to Mandy's lips and watched as the girl managed two sips. She set the glass down.

'It's been a great worry you've been, my dear. And Himself up and down the stairs like a wounded bear! Why, he even threatened Dr Hinson, and a finer man than the doctor you never saw in your life. Threatened to cut off his—er—to do him a great damage if he lost you, he did! This old house hasn't seen the like since his grandfather died!' She held up the glass again, and Mandy managed two more sips.

The girl lay back in the bed and smiled. So much to have happened in one night, she thought. Wouldn't it have been nice if he—Mr Stone, that was—had been the one she loved? Which certainly was a ridiculous thought. Nobody, but nobody, fell in love in one night—or on one kiss. At least, sensible Amanda Small would not! Such a terrible temper he had! She filed the thought away in her eidetic memory and sighed. There were just too many puzzles to be solved. She sighed again, and faded away in sleep.

The next time she woke it was dark outside, and a tiny lamp kept vigil by her bed. The dog was still there, and came instantly to attention when she moved. Mandy manoeuvred her heavy hand over to it, and scratched at the scruff of the animal's neck. There was a figure sprawled in the chair near the window. Brian, fast asleep.

She turned her head to study him in the dim light. He wasn't exactly tall, just big. His hair was cut short, and looked to be a cross between straw after early harvest and the darker sand of Winchester beach. His eyebrows were heavy, and almost joined across the bridge of his Roman nose. Asleep he looked young and vulnerable. She remembered in great detail how forceful he was when awake!

Mandy reached out a hand towards him, and noticed that she was wearing a white cotton nightgown, sprigged with yellow roses. It was cut low, leaving her shoulders bare. It was also semi-transparent, she discovered, as she looked down at herself. It wasn't just her shoulders that looked bare! Lovely, lovely, she thought, and giggled soundlessly.

The dog stood up. It had been sitting on the floor, resting its head on the covers. Now, standing, it thumped its forelegs on the bed and began licking her arm with a rough tongue. Such an amazing size! A cat or two had wandered into Amanda's rose garden, but no dogs. This one was more in the order of a small pony. Her mind clicked through all the pictures of dogs that she had ever seen. Great Dane! She smiled at the animal, and hitched herself close enough to scratch behind its ears. The dog shifted its tongue-action to her face. Mandy squirmed under the rough ministration. The noise alerted the sleeper. He opened one eye, took in the situation, and jumped towards the bed.

'Get down, Liza,' he commanded. 'Get down, you monstrous idiot!'

The dog turned its massive head in its master's direction. Mandy threw her arms around Liza's head and clutched the massive frame to her breast. The dog resumed, licking anything it could reach. Brian chuckled as he moved her arms away and pulled the animal to the floor.

'I'm sorry, Amanda. It's never happened before, and I don't really understand why it's happening now. Liza isn't a house pet, she's an outdoor type. She usually sticks to my heels wherever I go. But for the last six days she's been sitting by your bed day and night, and nothing we could do would make her move. How do you feel?'

She smiled up at him and formed an OK sign with her finger and thumb. Her throat was dry, and her mind was still a little hazy. Six days? He offered her a glass with a straw sticking out of it. She sucked up the welcome fluid eagerly. Lemon and lime juice. When the glass was empty he set it aside, then used a paper towel to wipe her chin. 'Would you like to sit up for a few minutes?'

She nodded. He plumped up two pillows against the headboard, then grasped her gently under the armpits and raised her to a sitting position. The movement unsettled her stomach, and she gasped. The room seemed to rock, but regained its balance when he put his hands on her shoulders. She looked around.

Queen of all I survey, she giggled hysterically to herself. The room was spotless. The bed fittings gleamed pure white, just matching her gown—which, she suddenly remembered, was not all that much cover! She gulped and slid the blanket up a bit higher, trying to make it look like a casual move. He noticed, and grinned as he handed her a pencil and pad.

Thoughts, feelings, crowded in on her, but she was still too weak to think straight. Put everything aside, she commanded herself. Think only about the here and now, not *him*. Dear lord, not him!

'We'll have you something more to drink in a minute,' he said.

She snatched at the pad. 'Six days?' she wrote.

'Yes, six days,' he said quietly. 'The dance was last Saturday night, and today is Friday. You've had a hard time, little girl. Dr Hinson diagnosed flu, exhaustion, shock, and pneumonia. But I think all the crises are past. Your fever is gone. All in all, it's been quite a week.'

She shook her head and sighed. There it was again. Little girl! Well, why did she care if he thought she were a little girl? Somewhere in the back of her mind a memory stirred. Child, he had kept saying, and to prove to him that she was *not* a child, she had stood up in front of the fireplace and—oh, no! Her face flushed a brilliant red, and the two freckles on the tip of her nose stood out. Oh, no, I couldn't have done that!

'There's nothing to worry you,' he continued, blaming her blush on things present rather than things past. 'I still haven't been able to contact your parents. Dr Hinson is the only one in the county who seems worried about Amanda Small, and he hasn't had the time to tell me anything at all about you.' He stopped talking and looked down at her, only to find her staring back at him, wide-eyed. 'Amanda?' he prompted. 'Your parents?'

Nobody but *you* and Dr Hinson worries about me, she thought, and savoured it. 'Parents dead,' she wrote. 'Mrs Purcell went to her sister in Newport.'

'Is she an aunt or something?' he asked.

'Housekeeper,' she wrote. It was too hard to explain on such a small pad. And explanations about Mrs Purcell required some careful thinking. Besides, he didn't have to know. Not yet, at least!

'You don't have any living relatives?'

He sounded astonished. Evidently he must come from a big family, she thought. But if that is so, where are they? And how about me? What about the hospital people? Or the Red Cross? Or the library, where I do volunteer work? Surely *somebody* must have missed me? Oh, lord, what I need is a relative. A close, loving relative!

A tear formed in the corner of her eye. She stifled it. People like Amanda Small just didn't cry, she insisted to herself. She ducked her head so he might not see the tear in her eye.

He opened his mouth to make a comment, but Mrs Duggan came in carrying a dish of warm soup on a tray. The housekeeper shooed him out of the room, wrapped a large towel around Mandy's throat to protect her nightgown, and then spoon-fed her. Mandy's stomach made protesting noises, but she managed to hold it all down. Mrs Duggan gave her a special sort of cherishing smile, helped her to the bathroom, then resettled her in bed and began to brush out her bronze curls. Mandy was asleep by the tenth stroke.

The housekeeper slid her down into the bed again without awakening her, and went out. Liza, who had been lying down in the hall, came in and resumed her guardianship. Mandy stirred from time to time, restless, but throughout the night there was a magnificent smile on her face.

Three days later she was strong enough to get up out of the bed by herself. Two more and she was able to go downstairs and wander cautiously about. She was embarrassed at first because of a lack of clothes, but eventually three sets of jeans and blouses appeared at her bedside and, content with these, she began to explore. Only one door was closed to her: the door of Brian's workroom.

'You mustn't bother Himself when he's working,' Mrs Duggan explained as they shared a cup of coffee in the kitchen. 'This farm hasn't paid its keep in twenty years. He supports us all by his writing. And when things don't go right, he throws things. A nasty temper, Himself has, if I do say so, *acushla*.'

'What does he write?' Mandy scribbled on the kitchen slate.

'Anything that makes money,' Mrs Duggan laughed, 'but mostly adventure stories filled with big buxom blondes. Anything that will turn a dollar. And, believe me, he turns a lot of them.'

Mandy's trim body shook with her silent giggles, but her mind was turning over at full speed. He had a terrible temper? Well, nobody was perfect, right? If throwing things relieved his mind, then why not? A terrible crash came from the workroom at that moment, punctuating the conversation.

'Oh, dear,' Mrs Duggan wailed. 'That's his tape recorder. We don't have many of them left. Just in case, I'd better get another from the cupboard.'

Wow! He throws things with a vengeance, Mandy thought. Correction! He throws *expensive* things with a vengeance. If that's the way he is—Himself is—this morning, I'd better whistle out of sight!

She slipped off the kitchen stool and wandered down the hall, past the workroom and the study, to the door of what, in the old days, would have been called a drawing-room. It was the piano that caught her attention. A gleaming black Steinway baby grand. It drew her like a magnet. She peered around carefully to be sure she was alone, and then hurried to the instrument. She lifted the lid, arranged herself on the commodious bench seat, tried her foot on the pedals, and softly ran a scale.

The instrument was in perfect condition, well-tuned in an area of the world where salt dampness made piano-tuning a major problem. Without thought she flexed her fingers and the lovely little Viennese waltzes that she favoured permeated the atmosphere. She played for half an hour, until her unpractised wrists grew tired, then she segued into the sweetness of 'Clair de Lune'. It was not until the last note had sounded and her hands were resting reflectively on the keys that the great dog sitting behind her nudged her back with its cold nose.

Mandy turned around and bowed from the waist as Liza watched with those liquid brown eyes. Her relationship with the dog had developed strangely. The animal had guarded her until she left the bedroom, and then disappeared. From time to time, though, day and night, Liza would pad up to Mandy, look her over carefully, then disappear. A sort of game had also evolved. Whenever Brian wanted Mandy he would send the dog for her and, as now, Liza would gently take Mandy's wrist in her mouth and lead her to where he waited. In this instance he was in the study.

'A drink?' he enquired. She shook her head. Alcohol had never been her thing. Besides, if he was as angry as the noises indicated, she wanted to keep all her wits about her. But he didn't seem to be the least bit angry. In fact, he was wearing that boyish smile.

'It's just lemon and lime juice,' he coaxed. 'Mrs Duggan seems to be on a lemon and lime kick, and I never dare say a word. Good cooks are hard to find!'

I'll just bet you never say a word, she thought. If anyone around here ever did a single tiny thing you didn't like, I'll bet you would roar the house down! She accepted a glass of juice, on the 'better be safe than sorry' theory. Besides, she was a little bit thirsty.

'You play well,' he commented. 'I think everybody in the house stopped to listen. With practice you could go on to big things.' He smiled at her as he raised his glass in salute. She shook her head and looked for a convenient pad. They seemed to be appearing in every room in the house lately.

'No,' she wrote, 'my hand span is too small. I can never really get any better.'

He searched her face for some sign of regret. Most people he knew would have been depressed by the idea. But not this girl. It was a fact that her hands were too small for major concert work. She had accepted that fact and gone on. Her sunny smile dispelled any other thoughts he might have had.

'Well, what I want to talk to you about,' he continued, 'is that I've finally located your Mrs Purcell. When she heard the news she said she would be back tomorrow, early. If you feel up to it we'll drive over about eleven o'clock tomorrow, and you can be in your own home at last. How's that?'

He expected a smile of pleasure from her. It wasn't there. He had taken her so completely by surprise that she was unable to mask her feelings. Surely it would be wonderful to see the old house where she had grown up? And the rose garden. But for some reason it no longer seemed like 'going home'.

Home is here, her conscience nagged at her. Right here where I'm standing now. And if I go back to Tickle Street, will I ever see him again? Her face crumbled at the thought.

He sensed her feelings and pulled her close, up against the soft warmth of his cardigan, his hand running up and down her back. 'What is it, Amanda? Don't you *want* to go home?' The answer was too complex for her pencil to handle. She moved back away from him and did her best to explain it in American Standard sign-language. He threw up his hands in despair.

'I don't understand a bit of it!' he laughed. 'I'll have to learn. And if you don't really want to go home, we'll visit together tomorrow. If it's all that bad you can come back with me. All right?'

And *that* just saved a thousand miles of writing. She sighed. He was waiting for an answer. She looked up at him, smiling, and nodded. 'I thank you for everything,' she signed.

'If that means thank you, why, you're very welcome,' he said as he kissed her forehead. A warm feeling ran up her spine as she wiggled closer to him—for a moment, of course. Just one heart-warming moment.

The next day was sunny and warm. They made the trip in his tiny MG, with Liza squatting behind them between the luggage rack and the front seats. The top was down, and the wind played with Mandy's cap of curls. She glowed. When they turned the corner on to Tickle Street she began to see familiar sights, and when they rounded the bend leading down towards the harbour, she tugged at Brian's arm and gestured off to the right, where the old house sat majestically among its trees. He pulled up at the main gate, and got out.

Independent little Amanda began to scramble out herself, then remembered her manners and waited for him to come around. He was *definitely* laughing at her as he helped her out of the bucket seat, but the day was too nice for her to lose her temper. She led him through the gate and up the front path. The little signpost was still out front, with both her mother's and her father's name-plates hanging there. She never intended to take them down. She stopped for a second, just for luck, and knocked her forefinger on the wooden post.

There was no need to ring the bell. The door flew open before they climbed the two front steps, and Mrs Purcell stood there, her gaunt figure masked by her loose black dress. Her white hair was pulled back tightly in a bun.

'Well,' she said, 'I knew you'd get in trouble going to that dance. I told you, but you wouldn't listen, would you?'

Mandy stopped at speaking distance. Her hands moved in signed English as she simultaneously mouthed the words, 'It wasn't the dance. The dance was perfect. But after it was all over I was caught in the rain. I caught pneumonia——' she had to slow down and spell the word, letter by letter '——Mr Stone put me in his bed, and he nursed me, and called the doctor, and was very kind.'

Mrs Purcell frowned back. 'I told you so,' she repeated. 'No good never come of dancing. And you spent time in his bed? What about that, Mr——?' Her eyes were bleak as she stared at Brian over Mandy's head, a stare that indicated the explanation had better be very good.

Evidently Brian was experienced in reading *this* sort of sign language. Mandy backed up against him, shaken by the coldness of her welcome. He put a hand on her shoulder, as if he could feel it too. 'My name is Stone. I'd be happy to tell you about it.' His deep voice resonated through the empty hall behind them. Mandy could see that the housekeeper was impressed. 'We put Mandy in my room because it has its own bathroom,' he began. 'I sat in a chair by the window for half the time. Mrs Duggan, my housekeeper, sat there the other half of the time. And what little sleep I managed was acquired on an old horsehair sofa out in the hall—which I got rid of today, by the way. I take it you're Mrs Purcell?'

'Yes, I am.' And then, remembering her manners, 'Please come in.' She gestured and stepped aside to allow him entry. As Mandy followed, Mrs Purcell signed to her, 'No good will ever come of this!'

They shared coffee in the small kitchen. Nothing else was offered. 'I don't have time to be fancy,' Mrs Purcell said. 'I've raised Amanda since she was fourteen. What do you do for a living, Mr Stone?'

He recognised the inquisition for what it was, and accepted the challenge. 'I'm thirty-two years old. I write books for a living. It's a steady job. Last year I paid taxes on ninety-eight thousand dollars. My father and mother are retired and living in Hawaii. I have two married sisters, one unmarried aunt, and two dogs!'

Mandy watched Mrs Purcell's face carefully. Good lord, she thought, he's on his best behaviour. But suppose he loses his temper? She placed a tentative hand on his arm. He smiled at her, and patted her hand. 'And oh, yes, I'm unmarried—what do they say around here— I'm not spoken for. Now, does that raise any problems?'

'There is a problem,' Mrs Purcell returned. There was a high-pitched whine in her voice. 'I was hired to supervise and keep house until Amanda was twenty-one years old. And now that time is past.'

'What are you saying?' he asked in amazement. 'Are you telling me that's all it was? Just a job? And now you're finished with it?' Amanda squeezed his arm again. There was no doubt about it—he was getting more and more angry.

Mrs Purcell had the grace to blush. 'Well, we ain't related. It's hard raising a—a handicapped kid. And now my sister is sick. She'll probably require an operation. And there's the three kids. All under ten, they are. I can't be in two places at once, and blood is thicker than water. Amanda's old enough to take care of herself——'

'It sounds as if Amanda has been taking care of herself for a long time,' he interrupted coldly. 'I have the answer to the problem. The child has been settled and happy at my house for a couple of weeks. So you can plan to go right back to your sister. Pack Mandy's things so she can come back with me.'

'I was promised a five-hundred-dollar bonus,' Mrs Purcell insisted grimly. 'A cash bonus at the end of the job. I ain't going without it!'

'Amanda?' He looked the question at her. She nodded her head, and fumbled for her pencil. 'But I haven't the money right now,' she scribbled.

'Forget it,' he answered gruffly. He dipped into his pocket and pulled out a cheque-book. 'Five hundred dollars?' He tore the cheque out and handed it to Mrs

Purcell. She snatched it and scanned it quickly before folding it up and tucking it into her pocket. She was suddenly smiling now, a smile that looked as if it might leave cracks in her face.

'There's a bus out of the village at five o'clock to-night,' she simpered. 'I'll go and pack for Amanda. Why don't you go out back with her and look at her rose garden?'

'*Her* rose garden?' he queried.

'Yes. I never could get the girl to take an interest in proper things, like church, and sewing, or social mixing. All she wanted to do was stay home and work in her rose garden.'

Mandy stamped her foot in anger, defiance, embarrassment. The rose garden had been the source of endless small arguments over many years. Her face flushed, and she was about to sign an argument when Brian came around behind her, picked her up by the waist, and swung her up in his arms.

'Now, which way to the garden?' he asked jovially. Mrs Purcell, shocked, pointed a finger at the back door. Mandy kicked and squirmed for a moment—for dignity's sake, no more—and they were on the back porch.

Whatever he had expected, this was not it. A remarkably startled Brian restored Mandy to her feet and stared down into the sunken garden. Almost a quarter of an acre of enclosed ground, it was designed as a circle within a square. The square was a brick wall about six feet high. The circle was a white pebbled path which completely enclosed a tremendous flower garden. At the centre of the circle he could see the roof of a small white gazebo, partly hidden by trees and the riot of flowers. Two tiny paths meandered through and around the flower-beds. The flowers themselves were in no formal order, their beds scattered and curved as the heart dictated. Ramblers climbed trellises against the gazebo. Blooming quadrants of ivory floribunda canes sprang up here and there, and tiny patches of golden apricot hybrid tea-roses added colour. One whole bed was given over to the orange-blended grandiflora. And the heavy scent was provided by a sweeping narrow bed of damascenes, for the more modern the hybridisation, the less the scent.

Around the outside perimeter of the flower jungle were beds of other flowers. Tulips now past their prime. Tiger-lilies, light with blooms, begonias, and one bed entirely devoted to pansies and geraniums. In three of the four corners of the garden, up against the brick wall, were set a red maple, a Japanese cherry tree, and furthest from the house, near a small stream, a weeping willow. The fourth corner consisted of a small rock garden, down which the little stream fell as a waterfall. The back wall, directly facing them, was crowded with lilacs, their blossoms long since lost. 'Holy Harry,' he muttered. 'I take it all back, Amanda. It's stupendous. You did it all yourself?'

She smiled up at him, happy in his acknowledgement, but the truth pushed her to qualify it all. She took out her little notebook. 'I hired a man to do the heavy work,' she wrote.

'Wow!' He shook his head from side to side. 'Boy, did I ever have you figured wrong, right from the start.' She tugged at his hand and led him down the steps and up the wandering path that led to the gazebo.

Her little white metal table stood at its centre, with two matching wire chairs that suddenly seemed too dainty for him. She gestured towards the padded wooden bench that followed the angles of the octagonal gazebo. He stopped at the table, thumbing through the books she had left there. He picked up a couple of them, read the titles, then put them back.

'Child psychology, in German?' he asked. She nodded. 'You speak German? Oh, no, what a stupid question.' He whacked himself on the forehead with his open palm. 'I meant do you *read* German?'

Mandy fumbled through the papers on the desk and found a large notepad. 'I read German,' she wrote. 'I was a part-time student at the University of South-eastern Massachusetts. I'm interested in children, and flowers, and lots of other things.'

He shook his head, a wry smile on his face. 'Give me a *for-instance*; what else can you do?' For a moment she almost told him. Almost explained how her cheerless childhood had driven her into intellectualism; how she spent countless nights at the university, following her own learning whims. Almost, she might have told him. But there was a cautionary note in the back of her mind.

Men didn't marry beautiful minds, they married beautiful bodies! Where had she heard that? On that interview on public television, with a famous dean of women. A lively intellectual lady, who had sounded just a little bitter when she'd said it!

But there *was* something she could tell him. Something perfectly innocuous, something that a girl could do without appearing to be an 'intellect'. She laughed up at him silently, stood there for a minute with her hands behind her back, then pulled them out in front of her, palms down, and wiggled her fingers.

'Piano? I already knew that.'

She shook her head and frowned at him, then repeated the movement. 'Typewriter?' he guessed.

She gave him another smile and fumbled for her pad. 'Secretarial training,' she wrote. 'Type fifty words a minute. Shorthand not that good.'

'Marvellous damn hell!' he roared. 'I've been screaming for a week because that idiot secretary of mine quit, and here I've had one living in my house all that time. Amanda—would you work for me?'

Oh, lord, she thought instantly. The best or the worst. I'd love to work for him—or would I? He roars at people. I think he thinks he keeps slaves. Maybe he'll want something more than typing! And I don't know beans about things like that. *If* I work for him, will he come to think of me as the nice girl I am? The *very* nice girl I am? But, of course, I'm no raving beauty, so maybe he wouldn't even *think* about... And, having thought about both sides of the question, and finding them equally attractive, she blushed red as a beet.

'Will you?'

Yes, she mouthed at him. Might as well start him off right. He has to learn lip-reading, or sign-language, or both! But—she reached for her pad again. 'I can't answer the telephone,' she wrote gloomily.

'Who cares?' he shouted. 'Just think! For my very own! A secretary who can't talk back, and who does what she's told! Get with it, girl!'

And that's the core of it, Amanda told herself disgustedly as they walked back to the house. He wants a girl who does what she's told. A sweet, biddable thing. Well, Amanda Small, you can't have your cake and eat it too. If that's what it takes, behold argumentative, independent Amanda, learning to be a most biddable young lady!

They were back in the car by four o'clock, having made their goodbyes. Mrs Purcell unbent enough to let Mandy kiss one cold cheek, and then Brian was stuffing her back into the overloaded MG. 'And you lived with her for seven years?' he muttered as he climbed into the car.

It took longer to go home than it had to come. With all the luggage there was no place for Liza to sit. So Brian drove the car at a brisk five miles an hour, and the huge dog loped along beside them, looking as if she could devour the car with two bites. As they came into the house, Mrs Duggan came out.

'Supper's on the table,' she said. 'And I have to hurry along. My father isn't well today. Is Mandy going to stay here?' That last after she surveyed the pile of luggage in the back of the car.

Mandy nodded excitedly. He confirmed it in clipped tones, and a frown furrowed Mrs Duggan's normally cheerful face. She took her employer's arm and led him aside for a quick conference. Even at a distance Mandy could see him blush. It startled her. She didn't think men did that sort of thing, but there it was. His almost-blond hair was wind-ruffled, and an occasional hank of hair fell down over his forehead. His bush jacket displayed wide shoulders and strong arms. Where the sleeve ended, just level with his gold watch-band, she could see some of the heavy mat of hair on his arms. And his face was a bright red.

Evidently the two of them came to some agreement. Mrs Duggan waved cheerfully and went on down the stairs. Brian came back to Mandy, took her arm, and hurried her down the hall into the study. He went over to the desk and sat down, picking up the telephone. Mandy went with him, dropping on to the stool adjacent to his chair.

He leaned over and ruffled her curls. 'I forgot about propriety,' he said, 'and Mrs Duggan gave me both barrels. You're not a child, Mandy.'

'Well, thank heaven he's finally got *that* right, she told herself as she watched him dial a nine-digit number. While he waited for the circuit to be established, he said, 'Mrs Duggan is only here days. Her father requires a certain amount of nursing. He's eighty-seven. And she can't be here on weekends. Now how in the world can you and I live here together without ruining your reputation, my girl?'

She sat up cautiously and moved her stool an inch or two away from him. Ruin her reputation? How could he do that? But Brian had already turned to the telephone. She wanted to tell him that she didn't think he could ruin her reputation. She wanted to tell him that she was fiercely independent. She wanted to tell him— and that was the core of the problem. There was no way in the world she could tell him. Her face paled. During the time she was in the children's hospital they had tried to teach her that she was *not* handicapped; that indeed she was like everyone else, except she spoke a different language. She had sailed through her girlhood secure in that thought. By and large everyone she had dealt with had made some effort to understand *her* language. But the adventures of the last few days had left her confused and insecure. And here she was, at the most critical point in her life, weighed down by the fear that her 'handicap'—and how she hated that word—might make it impossible for her to tell him everything she wanted him to know!

He was concentrating on the telephone, and didn't notice her anguish. The number he dialled was ringing. He pushed another button on the telephone and set it back down in its cradle. She could hear the ringing, now coming from a little amplifier on his desk. She cuddled an inch closer. Close enough for his hand to caress her curls again. It was an electronic telephone, and she would be able to hear both sides of the conversation. A woman answered.

'Hello, Aunt Rose,' he said in a normal speaking voice. 'It's Brian calling.'

'Brian?' The voice sounded sceptical. 'You haven't called me in two years, you young devil. How are you?'

'I'm fine, Aunt Rose, but I have this small problem.'

'Don't we all, young man? Why else would you call me?'

'Aunt Rose, do you suppose you could give up your whist games for a while? I need you up here in Massachusetts.'

'Now that's asking a great deal, Brian. You want me to give up my entire Florida lifestyle and fly north just for you?'

'That's about the size of it,' he admitted. 'I need you pretty badly.'

'Is there something wrong with your housekeeper— Mrs Duggan, it was? I'm not much of a housekeeper, and I don't do windows.'

'No, Aunt Rose, there's nothing wrong with Mrs Duggan. It's just that I've—well, you won't believe it.' He sounded positive that she wouldn't! 'I've worked myself into a corner, up here, Aunt Rose, and I need a live-in chaperon.'

There was silence on the line for a moment, then a gale of laughter. 'I think there must be something wrong with this telephone connection. You need a what?'

'Don't fool around,' he replied sombrely. 'I'm in a jam. I need a chaperon.'

Again that pregnant pause. 'Brian, if any of my other nephews had called and said that, I'd understand. But you? You started chasing skirts at fourteen and haven't quit yet!'

'Please—Aunt Rose!' He was beginning to lose his temper. Mandy carefully moved away from him, prepared to duck. It was such a delightful conversation so far! 'There's someone else listening,' he continued. 'It's an emergency. Honestly, I need a chaperon. Will you come?'

'Is the girl there? Let me speak to her.'

'She's here, but she can't talk.'

'Well, take your hands away from her mouth and let me talk to her.'

'Aunt Rose! Damn it, Aunt Rose, she can't speak to you. She's unable to speak to you!'

'Hmmph,' his aunt snorted. 'A likely story.' Another pause. 'I'm really expecting guests down here. I invited a young couple that both you and I know. They're coming over from Paris after the racing season.'

'So you could invite them to come up here,' he replied quickly. 'The weather is nice, the beach is open, and I'll even get the swimming-pool cleaned up. Please come?'

'Oh, my,' his aunt laughed, 'I can actually hear a tremor in your voice. Can it be that the great wolf of New England has met his match? How intriguing. And she can't talk to me? That's the hook in your plot, isn't it? You knew I could never resist a mystery. When shall I come?'

'Tomorrow,' he said, then waited for the objections. None came. 'Early tomorrow. Wire me the flight number and I'll meet you in Providence.' The phone clicked and went dead.

He shook his head, then turned to look at Mandy. She had moved away again, watching his eyes. Beautiful eyes, she thought. Almost as nice as Liza's. But the dog loves me.

'I think that settles our problem, Amanda,' he said. 'Does it suit you?'

Oh, my, she thought, as her hands unconsciously balled into fists in her lap. Will that suit me? What the devil is teasing at me? Why is my hand shaking just now? Her thoughts were too many to write down, so she merely nodded her head.

He pulled her up to her feet with one hand, gave her a gentle pat on her bottom, and headed her for the stairs. 'You must be tired,' he said. 'Scrub up, we'll have a bite to eat, and then off to bed.'

CHAPTER FOUR

THE day's excitement left Mandy confused. She danced up the stairs, unpacked her clothes, showered, and wore her favourite pink floral-print minigown to bed. Sleep would not come. She tossed and turned, recalling every facet of the day. Everything that had happened started out with 'He—'.

Riding down the wind in his little car. Appreciation of her rose garden. Spiking Mrs Purcell's guns. Holding her close. Accepting her into his household! And all that's required in repayment is to do just what I'm told! At that she had to grit her teeth. I wonder how long little not-so-biddable Amanda is going to be able to grin and bear it! she asked herself. Not very long, her New England conscience answered.

There was one thing to watch; one thing she already agreed to sacrifice. It might be nice, living in the Stone house. So no more mention of intellectual Amanda Small. Men had tremendous egos which had to be pampered, or so her friends all said. Intellectual women need not apply. It was no wonder, when she finally fell asleep, that she was awash in an Edwardian dream, locked up in an old English manor, at the mercy of the wicked earl—and at that point everything dissolved into blackness.

She awoke slowly, in the grip of the same dream. The wicked earl had her by the wrist and was trying to drag her out of bed. Mandy pried one eye open, and the cruel earl disappeared, to be replaced by Liza. The dog's mouth was locked securely around Amanda's right wrist, but gently enough so the massive teeth did not mark her skin.

She managed one quick look at her bedside clock. Ten o'clock! She had promised Brian that she would be ready to work by eight at the latest! She swung back the blankets with her free hand and stuffed her feet into her slippers. The dog would not allow a detour through the bathroom, but kept urging her towards the door.

I can't go down dressed like this, she thought, but Liza kept tugging. And since the animal weighed almost as much as she did, it wasn't a fair fight. Besides, she warned herself, their friendship hadn't been tested. Who knew what the dog would do if she resisted? Mandy shrugged her shoulders. She didn't mind a battle, but only a fool went into one in which she was a sure loser. She snatched up her housecoat with her free hand, and followed along as best she could.

The dog thumped down the stairs, with Mandy in tow, and turned right, leading the way into the sunlit kitchen. At which point Liza considered her job done. She dropped Mandy's wrist and went off to lie under the kitchen table.

The room was silent, but it was the silence of a place where conversation had just come to an abrupt halt. Brian and an older man were sitting at the table. Mrs Duggan and a younger woman stood by the kitchen sink.

'Good lord, Amanda,' Brian hissed at her. 'Put something on!'

It was enough to remind her that in the bright sunlight her nightgown was practically transparent. She looked at him furiously and raised her right arm. He came instantly, took her wrist and examined it. Mrs Duggan came up on her other side, grabbed at her trailing housecoat, and hustled her into it.

'She didn't hurt you?' He sounded worried, and then embarrassed. 'I didn't send her!' Mandy smiled her acceptance of the implied apology.

'You might as well have,' interjected Mrs Duggan angrily. 'You walked into the kitchen as bold as brass, and you stomped around, and you roared, "Where's Mandy!" The dog doesn't know the difference between polite and angry. So she went off to find her!' The elderly housekeeper looked at him as if she wanted to fricassee him in oil!

Mrs Duggan was zipping up the housecoat as she talked. Mandy was too astonished to know whether to laugh or cry, whether to sit or run. The older man at the table was studying his shoelaces. The young girl was giggling. Mandy walked over to her. Brian made the introductions.

'Becky,' he said, putting his arm around the young blonde and pulling her forward. 'Becky helps Mrs Duggan in the house.' He moved over to the table and put a hand on the man's shoulder. 'Mr Rutherford,' he announced. The man got up, like an attenuated beanpole, unfolding. He stood inches taller than Brian, but would hardly cast a shadow except in the strongest sunlight. His weather-beaten face was crinkled into a broad smile. 'Mr Rutherford runs the farm, drives the car, fixes everything that breaks, and plays a lousy hand of poker.'

The man watched Mandy for a silent moment, then reached out an enormous hand to engulf her own. 'How d'ye do,' he said, and sat down again. Brian motioned Mandy to a chair.

'Another cup of coffee?' he asked Rutherford. 'Our girl needs to have her breakfast?'

'T'warnt do no harm,' the older man allowed. Becky came over with the coffee-pot while the housekeeper busied herself with the frying-pan. They sipped without conversation. When his second cup was finished, Rutherford stood up again.

'Ain't much for conversation, be you?' he enquired. And, without waiting for an answer, 'That's good. Ain't nothin' worse than a cacklin' female.' He stomped to the door. 'Ain't much for words myself,' he chuckled. 'You come see the farm be you a mind to.' He walked out.

Mrs Duggan came over to the table with a plate of bacon and eggs. 'First time I ever heard Caleb talk free with a woman,' she observed with a chuckle. 'You made a hit with that one, Amanda.'

'Of course, he doesn't see many women waltzing into the kitchen half-naked either,' Brian snapped. Mrs Duggan put both hands on her hips and fried his guts with a single glance. He ducked his head.

'It's your dog that's responsible,' the housekeeper snapped. He ducked again.

'I really don't understand that dog,' he mused. 'For eight years she's been a good guard dog. Never one for feelings, was she?' He appealed to Mrs Duggan for support. She nodded agreement. 'And now all of a sudden she's taken to Amanda like a second skin. Do you have any idea what it's about, Mandy?'

She grinned at him and picked up the piece of chalk that went with the kitchen slate. 'Liza thinks that she is my mother,' she wrote. He shook his head in mock disgust. There was just a trace of a smile playing at the corners of that mobile mouth. Devil? Saint? Both at the same time? she asked herself.

'Come on, now, girl.' He interrupted her brief reverie with a tap on the shoulder. 'I've already filled two tapes for you to transcribe. We have to produce fifty thousand words before next Friday to pay the mortgage.'

She giggled at him silently, and got up from the table. He looked—dangerous. She sidled carefully by, being sure not to turn her back on him, and headed for the stairs. As she changed into her jeans she reviewed the conversation. All of it. There was so much she wanted to say—to him, to Mrs. Duggan, to everybody. And they couldn't speak her language. She looked down at her long, tapered fingers and wished it could be different. *I've got to be careful,* she thought. *I could fall in love with this man too easily. I must be some sort of masochist.*

He was in the workroom when she came down, sitting on the divan with his feet up, dictating another tape. He waved her to the typing table, where a playback machine and three tapes awaited her. She shook her head, already discouraged. It certainly did not compare with typing *thank you* notes for the Red Cross!

'What's the matter?' he asked, stopping his dictation in mid-sentence.

She looked over at him. 'I love you,' she signed.

'Thank me for what?' he asked. She turned her back to hide the suspiciously wet gleam in her eyes. 'All that——' he pointed towards the tapes '—has to be done in a hurry.' He jumped up from the divan. The tape recorder, which had been precariously balanced on his chest, crashed to the floor. He said a few choice words. They were words Mandy had heard on occasion, but didn't know how to spell. *At least I'll expand my vocabulary,* she told herself. But she managed to school her give-away face before she turned to him again.

'I said, that's what we have to do,' he repeated belligerently. 'Aren't you really interested?'

The male ego again, she sighed, and made a mental note. A slow smile spread across her face. She clasped her hands behind her back and rocked back and forth on her heels, trying to look intensely interested, but only managing to look extremely feminine.

'What we *really* have to do,' he said in a more normal voice, 'is have one hour of instruction every day in sign-language, starting now.'

He crossed his arms in front of him and stared back at her, as if daring her to disagree. But since teaching sign-language was one of the things she did regularly, she snapped her fingers to get his attention, and started out on the first lesson. Being very careful, of course, to avoid phrases like 'I love you,' or 'thank you,' or 'good morning.'

At eleven o'clock on the nose he called a halt. 'My fingers feel like a plate of cooked spaghetti,' he complained. 'How am I doing, teach?'

'Excellently,' she signed. 'What do I do now?'

'Get to work, of course,' he growled. 'Did you think this was a holiday?' And before she could think of a snappy answer he turned his back, cutting off all hope of communication.

'Rat,' she signed at his unresponsive back. 'Double dyed and dipped in cold molasses!'

Watch what you're doing, Amanda Small, she lectured herself as she bent over the typing desk. He's no fool. He looks like a great big cuddly bear, but he's got a sharp mind and a bad temper to match!

Despite all her wishing, the tapes had not got up and gone away. They still lay there, glaring balefully at her. Finish us! they demanded. At once! She stuck out her tongue at them. She didn't really mind trying to be biddable with him, but no second-rate sound tape was going to give *her* orders!

She pulled up a typing chair, adjusted its height and back position, and inserted the triple-ply paper into the electronic typewriter. She flexed her fingers to loosen them up, then slipped the headset over her ears and began to copy. The first two sentences slipped by her completely. She rewound the tape and concentrated. He dictated slowly, and acted out the dialogue, using a different voice for each part. The story was interesting, a spy-thriller about an English female agent who had come to St Tropez to wheel and deal in secrets. The words began to flow from her ears to her fingers. But as she typed, the story swept her up.

That was until she got to chapter two, when her face began to turn more and more red as the story-line developed. Until at last, unbelieving, she stopped and glared at him over the top of the typewriter. She realised that the market called for sexy spies—but three different men in the same afternoon?

'I don't need an editor,' he snapped at her. 'Just a typist.' She gulped, switched the machine back on, and let her fingers take command of things. They did, at a slow thirty words a minute, shutting out everything and everybody in the room. When he touched her on the shoulder she stopped in surprise. The wall clock read two o'clock, and she had finished two of the three tapes. He untangled the headset from her hair and pulled her to her feet.

'Lunchtime,' he said. 'You need to let that machine cool off. I don't believe I've ever heard a typewriter go for so long. Is it all in English?' She handed him one of the completed pages for inspection. He pursed his lips. 'Not one mistake,' he said in awe. She grinned at him and patted the self-erase key on the typewriter. He stretched, like a great mountain cat. She could not suppress a look of—well—admiration. He shook his head sadly, and tilted her chin up with two fingers.

'Don't make the mistake of falling in love with your boss,' he said softly. 'I can read your face like a book, child. You're too young for romancing with men like me. It would probably be only a schoolgirl crush, anyway. Not that I totally object. Even the best of us can use some unadulterated hero-worship now and then. But you need more experience before you play in my league.'

There he goes again with that child business, she raged to herself. You're too young to—you need more—damn him! She picked up pad and pencil with a trembling hand. 'You mean I need more experience with men?' she wrote.

'Yes,' he responded, grinning.

'I don't really know many men,' she scribbled. 'Would you give me some names? Would Mr Rutherford do?' Her eyes searched his solemnly. She was getting better at camouflaging her emotions.

He slapped his hand hard against his trouser leg. 'Damn it, Mandy, are you trying to make me feel like a fool on purpose? I didn't mean a word of what I said. No, Mr Rutherford won't do. And no, I don't want you wandering around the countryside getting more experience. Forget what I said. I've got to start guarding my tongue around here. You take everything I say as gospel truth, don't you?'

She nodded slowly, startled by what she had just discovered about herself. It wasn't a joke, something she had made up and kept to herself these past few days.

She *did* love him. Lord only knew when it had started, but there it was, today, full-blown, tearing at her heart with an intensity she had never felt before. No matter how *he* felt, or what he said, she loved him. Oh, lord, she sighed to herself, why couldn't it have been just an infatuation? She could feel a blush stealing up to her cheeks as she stared helplessly up at him.

He leaned over and gently kissed her on the lips. 'Come on,' he coaxed. 'Lunch break.'

After a light lunch they went walking, 'for relaxation,' he said. They strolled around the perimeter of the house, and he explained it all. The mansion was actually a rebuilt farmhouse. One that had suffered many atrocities in the rebuilding, including the addition of the ballroom.

'It was once a solarium,' he explained, as they looked down on the house from the top of the ridge. 'Then in the 1890s my grandfather went society-mad. He thought he could imitate all the multimillionaires in Newport. He was right in one sense. He finished the house just the way he wanted it. But he died broke.'

She offered him a tentative smile, and looked around her. Thackery Point was a high ridge of land that sloped down gently to a tidal river on one side, and dropped off precipitously into the Atlantic ocean on the other. The house was located below the top of the ridge, to provide shelter from the offshore winds. The near hillside was covered by apple orchards. Further away, to the south, stood fields of corn, fodder for the animals, which were the farm's main interest. But the garden, which, along with the swimming-pool, isolated the house from the orchard, was a disgrace. She pointed down towards it and shook her head.

'The garden?' he asked. 'I thought a wild garden might be attractive.' The sun was shining in Mandy's eyes, so she missed the teasing gleam in his as he said it. Like the cape to the bull, his statement was enough to send any reasonable gardener into a rage. She stamped her foot and glared at him.

'Shameful,' she signed.

'Hmmm?' he returned. 'That wasn't in the lessons this morning.'

She whipped out her little pad. 'Shameful!' she scribbled. In her anger she bore down hard, and broke the point of her last remaining pencil. He began to bellow with laughter. She held the pencil up grimly in front of her. This is the breaking-point, she told herself fiercely. I can't communicate with him! How in God's good world can we ever establish a relationship if I can't communicate with him?

'And so the conversation ends?' he teased. She looked glumly at him, all her concern showing in her eyes. 'Well, perhaps not,' he added. He swept her up in those long gentle arms of his and kissed her. It was enough to send her sky-rocketing in panic, but apparently affected him not one whit.

'So there,' he said as he released her. 'There are more ways to communicate than you think, Mandy. And now I'd better get scooting before Aunt Rose burns a flap off my hide. I did promise to pick her up in Providence today.' He plucked a long stalk of grass, and chewed on it as they made their way back to the house, hand in hand. Neither of them noticed the curtains at the kitchen window falling back into place.

'I told you so,' Mrs Duggan said triumphantly. Becky merely grunted. After all, at sixteen, Becky still nourished vague hopes that he might wait for *her* to grow up.

Amanda went straight to the workroom, her brains about the consistency of mush. He didn't even come in to say goodbye. The drive to Green Airport would take, at most, three quarters of an hour. But he could easily have come in. She wished and wished for him to come. It would have made her day to have him kiss her just once more.

She knew when he left. There were voices at the front door. Moments later Liza thumped into the room, sniffed around suspiciously, then lay down with her head on Mandy's feet.

She stopped typing and looked down. Thanks a lot, she thought rather huffily. If you suppose you're helping my typing by anchoring my feet to the floor, dog, you've got another think coming. Do you really think you could guard anything, you great big lump? Liza huffed at her. She leaned down to stroke the stiff brindle hair behind the dog's ears, and then went back to work.

She finished all the tapes by four o'clock, and stacked the manuscript pages neatly in the middle of his desk. The story hadn't been as bad as she expected. The lovely female spy had managed, by some very arcane techniques, to steal the secrets and still retain some small portion of her—virtue—at the same time. All of which caused Mandy to consider the absolute gall of a writer who offered such a solution. She mouthed for none of the world to hear, 'Ain't you got no shame, Brian Stone?'

It was a question bound to be answered tomorrow, when he started the next chapter. But that was a whole night and a day away! So she bustled around the room, tidying up the divan, emptying his ashtrays, rearranging the mass of reference books strewn on the table, desk, chairs and floor.

Between the cleaning urges, there were three trips to the front door, but the road down the hill was empty. Liza trailed her everywhere she went. Mitchell, Liza's son, got up when she stepped out on to the front porch, then lay down again when she left. She strolled back through the empty kitchen and picked up an apple from the basket. The tractor drove up outside the back door just as her teeth sank into the polished Delicious apple. Intrigued by the noise, she picked up her pad and pencil and went out into the back yard.

Mr Rutherford was standing by the tractor, checking the oil level in the engine. She snapped her fingers to get his attention. He turned around and smiled as she held out her pad. 'I apologise for my dress this morning,' she wrote.

He read the note, then pushed his old cap to the back of his head. 'T'ain't necessary,' he said. 'Them short dresses is popular, I hear tell. I may be old, but I ain't dead, little lady!' His eyes twinkled down at her and she laughed back at him. And then he became solemn. 'He needs sumpin' like you. Brian, I mean. He be a good man, lass. Here they comes.'

Mandy dashed for the front door. A heavy Lincoln Continental was coming up the drive. Liza poked along behind Mandy, growling protests at each step. They both skidded on the highly polished floor, and slid the last few paces to the door.

She stopped to catch her breath, pat her hair into worse confusion than it was, and smooth down her wrinkled blouse. I should have changed, she thought. I should have combed my hair and put on a clean dress, and— if he sees me now, I shall surely fall into a hole and pull it up over me! She backed away, but it was too late to run. The door swung open, letting in the breeze, the sunshine, and Aunt Rose.

Miss Rose Francesca Stone was not at all what Mandy had expected. She was a pert little creature, about five feet two, who carried herself erectly, like a reigning duchess. Her figure was neatly slender, and she dressed it simply but effectively. Only her silver hair marked her for membership in the senior set. She was the sort of woman who looked busy even while standing still. She peered at Amanda through gold-framed glasses, and walked a quarter-way around her to complete the inspection.

'So. Amanda Small,' she said. The voice was a soft, gentle contralto. 'You're the reason for my mad dash from Florida?'

Mandy blushed under her searching stare. It was hard to know what to do. She could bow, smirk, or stand frozen in place. Instead she smiled and stretched out her hand. Aunt Rose grasped it warmly, pulled the girl closer, and kissed her cheek.

'Brian, you rascal,' she called over her shoulder. He stalked up the stairs, wearing an expression about halfway between concern and laughter.

'You cold-blooded devil,' she told him. 'You've got a colossal nerve. The child can hardly be out of school. I ought to take a stick to you, young man. I should have years ago!'

He chuckled. 'Every family needs a maiden aunt. Now stop barking at me. Can't you see you're scaring the child?'

Aunt Rose looked keenly at Mandy. 'You may be right,' she said. 'Come along, girl.' She hooked her right hand in Mandy's elbow, and side by side they went down the corridor. 'I need a rest before dinner,' Rose said.

'Find me a room where I can put my feet up. And you say she's the perfect secretary, Brian?'

'None better,' he commented.

Well! I wish he could have told *me* that, Amanda thought. Just one nice word. But he did, her conscience chided her! Shut up, she commanded it. That was this morning—now it's afternoon! Which wasn't much of an argument, and so she abandoned it.

'And why didn't you tell me she was so young?' Aunt Rose bubbled.

'She's not as young as she looks,' he retorted. 'She had her twenty-first birthday just a couple of weeks ago.'

'And then why didn't you tell me she was so pretty?'

Brian stopped in mid-step, as if he had never considered the subject before. His aunt stopped too, watching him carefully.

'I guess I just never thought about it,' he confessed. 'I haven't seen all that much of her. I guess, to tell the truth, I forgot to look!'

Mutiny flared in Mandy's eyes. The nerve of the big oaf! There wasn't a man in the whole world who had seen as much of her as Brian had. Everything there was to see, for that matter! And he hadn't noticed? With flying fingers she began to sign a diatribe at him.

'Whoa,' he laughed. 'You'll sprain a finger if you don't watch out!'

'I'll sprain your whole head,' she signed, fit to be tied.

'Very interesting,' Aunt Rose interjected. 'Did you understand all that, Brian?'

'No,' he replied, 'but I'm learning. The trouble here is that so far she hasn't used a single word in my vocabulary.'

'Who's your teacher?'

'Mandy!'

'And you never noticed how pretty she is? Horse feathers!' Before either of the others could answer, Aunt Rose swept up to the top of the stairs. 'And another thing. You're pretty lucky, Brian—if you hadn't assured me what a sweet, biddable girl she is, I would have sworn she was ready to hit you just now!'

He gave Mandy a curious look and backed away from her. 'I'll bring the bags in from the car,' he told the girl. 'Why don't you go and help Rose settle down?'

Getting Rose settled required no effort at all. Before Mandy could make it up the stairs, their Florida visitor had poked through all the empty rooms, taken her choice, and made herself very much at home. When Brian wandered in with the bags he was quickly dismissed, and the two women set about the unpacking.

'You have such lovely things,' Mandy wrote on her pad after the work was finished.

'That's my *business*,' Aunt Rose returned. 'I've been a designer for forty years, my dear. Now, what about Brian?'

Mandy looked at her in surprise. 'What about Brian?' she scribbled on her pad.

Rose laughed. 'Don't think you're going to hide it from me. Don't you know that every girl between sixteen and sixty who meets Brian falls in love with him?' Aunt Rose came over to her, resting one veined hand on her shoulder. 'There's no need to hide it,' she said. 'I'm on your side. It's time this nephew of mine had a good hard set-down, and if you're the girl to try it, I'll help. Now scoot out of here. I need a rest, a bath, and dinner—in that order.'

Mandy ducked her head. There was a bitter taste in her mouth. You fool, she thought, you've just become the tail-ender in a queue that must stretch for a hundred miles. All beauties, probably, all able to talk to him, to sing—lord, what would he want with an incomplete woman?

The next ten days passed in an amiable fog for Mandy. The daily sign-language instruction became twice a day, with Brian showing uncanny ability to remember and execute. It relieved some of the strain on her conscience, and gave her an opportunity to really communicate. At the same time it reinforced her own warning to herself. This Mr Brian Stone was altogether too clever for her own good! Along with progress in the language, his book was rolling at high speed. They were now up to chapter eleven, where the young heroine seemingly had met her match in the person of a tall dark KGB colonel over lunch in Vienna. Mandy was still intrigued by it all, even though the lunch had already lasted for fifteen pages.

Aunt Rose had really settled in by this time. She spent her days roaming the area, reacquainting herself with people and places she had not seen for years. She spoke amiably with Mrs Duggan, as friend to friend. She made innumerable telephone calls to close and distant friends, blithely charging the bills to Brian's account. Mandy, who had taken over the bookkeeping, hoping to introduce some order into Brian's gypsy accounting methods, was taken aback by the size of the bills. But then two royalty cheques arrived in the mail, and the number of zeros in front of the decimal points did much to soothe her fears.

The older woman took the girl in hand, too. She checked the workroom every day to see how things were going. Often she would command a halt to the literary effort, and sweep Mandy off on a trip with her. Twice they went in the big car to Providence, where she coerced the girl into buying newer and more stylish clothes. Despite the fact she had lived in Florida for many years, the old lady knew exactly where to go and what to ask for.

In the evenings Rose would sit in the library with her feet up, knitting. Brian joined her every night, bringing his paper and a glass of his favourite cognac. After the third night Mandy joined them, arranging herself on a pillow by the hearth, out of range of the conversational bullets they fired at each other. Listening to Aunt Rose talk was like taking a bath in a fast-running mountain stream. The lady cast out a non-stop stream of chatter like the bow-wave on a ship. The girl's ears would perk up whenever the subject of Brian's childhood came up.

He would grin and bear it at times when he was under discussion, but more often would get up and walk out for a few minutes. Mandy treasured every word, and hardly noticed how the birdlike eyes of the older woman were following her reactions. All in all, Mandy was beginning to feel both welcomed and loved, not a month after she had first entered the old house. Which was about the right recipe for a catastrophe.

She had finished her typing early. The book was making satisfactory progress. Brian was in a good mood. Aunt Rose was singing around the house. And even Mrs Duggan could be seen to muster a smile. Dinner was to be something special, so Mandy covered her typewriter, straightened up the divan, and went upstairs to change and bathe.

She stripped off her working uniform—jeans and a blouse—and checked her wardrobe. For tonight she would wear one of the special dresses Aunt Rose had helped her to select. It was time to make a special effort. Special because Aunt Rose had been nagging her for three days.

'Improve the packaging if you want to sell the goods,' the old lady had said, down in the kitchen.

To which Mrs Duggan had laughed and added, 'If you've got it, flaunt it!' And, feeling somewhat like a side of beef on display at the market, Mandy had given in.

The particular dress she chose was a light coral pleated double-knit, with a stand-up collar at the back, and a deep V-neckline. She laid the dress out on the bed, admired it for a moment, then walked into the bathroom. Because hers was an integrated suite, she always left the bathroom door open. But in her hurry tonight she hardly noticed that the bedroom door was ajar also. She stepped out of her flats, peeled off her bikini briefs, and climbed into the welcome embrace of the shower. The warm water gradually soothed away her tiredness. Her soap smelled of English lavender. She used it liberally, then shampooed her mass of tight curls. Doing it brought a fond recall.

Just this morning she had become annoyed with one curl which was too long. It kept falling over her face into her eyes. When she stopped to deal with it, Brian laughed. She stuck out her tongue at him, and made scissor movements with her fingers and the recalcitrant curl.

'Don't do that,' he said quickly, reaching over to close her scissor-fingers. She looked at him, puzzled. 'Your hair,' he said. 'Don't ever cut your hair. I love it the way it is.'

The warmth of his response had given her a glow much larger than warranted. Is *that* how you manage men? she asked herself. You get them to forbid your doing something that you had never planned to do anyway?

Chuckling to herself, she picked up her pad and wrote, 'If you say so, Brian.'

He settled back in his chair as if he were master of the world. Lordly male gave command, biddable female obeyed! She had a difficult time swallowing the giggles that clogged her throat! Was that why her mother had always laughed? And now, in the warmth of the shower, the scene was recalled and the pleasure experienced again.

With shower and shampoo complete, she shut off the water, wearing nothing but a broad grin. One of the smaller towels served as a turban. But as she reached behind her for one of the larger bath towels she felt the all-too-familiar sloppy wetness as Liza came up behind her and grabbed her wrist. Oh, no, not now! Mandy sighed. She tried to command the dog, but, as usual, Liza was operating on her own programme.

Working carefully to avoid piercing her skin, the Great Dane compelled her out of the bathroom and into the bedroom. She struggled. Liza growled, and continued tugging. Mandy made one last desperate grab and managed to sweep up another bath towel, but was unable to wrap it around herself. Slowly the dog edged her out into the hall, down the length of the corridor, and into Brian's bedroom. The door was left half open behind them.

Liza towed her into the middle of the room, but, instead of dropping her wrist, held on to it. As a result, Mandy was forced to stand in one place, still dripping wet from her shower, struggling at the almost impossible task of covering herself with the towel, one-handed.

In the middle of her struggle, Brian's bathroom door opened, and he came into the bedroom, fresh from his own shower. A small towel barely draped his hips. 'My lord!' he exclaimed softly. 'Not that damn dog again.

Turn her loose, Liza. Down girl!' The dog growled and hung on to her grip. 'As God is my witness, Mandy,' he pleaded, 'believe me. I didn't send her. I didn't even mention your name. Down, Liza, dammit!'

There was a light knock on the door. Without waiting for an invitation, Aunt Rose came bustling in. At that same instant Liza dropped her hold on Mandy's wrist and lay down at the girl's feet.

'Brian,' Rose started to say, 'I've just got a call about—— ' and her mind registered what her eyes were reporting. Her face turned beet-red. 'Damn you, Brian,' she yelled at him, 'I told you to leave that little girl alone!'

'It's not what you think,' he blurted out.

'No, it never is, is it?' his aunt replied. 'I suppose you want to tell me that the dog is responsible?'

'Well, to be absolutely—oh, hell, who would believe it if I told you?'

'Certainly not I,' his aunt returned. 'Cover yourself, girl, you're dripping all over the rug!'

She turned back to her nephew. 'And as for you, you don't need a chaperon, you need a marriage licence. And you'd better get one quickly, you hear me?'

The two Stones stood glaring at each other across the bed. Mandy, feeling as if she had been run down by a ten-ton truck, flopped weakly down on to the bed and tried desperately to cover herself. The two of them were talking over her head, beyond her comprehension. She huddled into the bath towel, making a sarong out of it, and stared at them in complete bewilderment.

'Well?' Aunt Rose insisted.

'I'm thinking,' he returned grimly.

'You should have done your thinking hours ago, you rascal. It may not be important to you. A man can stand this sort of thing, I suppose. But what about this poor girl's reputation? I've already heard talk in the village about you two living up here together before I arrived. And now the fat's really in the fire. How will it look when Edward and his sister Meredith arrive here next week? They've booked a flight from Paris already. That's what I came to tell you.'

'Damn traitor,' Brian snarled as he threw his slipper at the dog. Liza growled back at him, and moved closer to Mandy. 'Edward and Meredith? Surely you don't mean the Clemsons, do you?'

Aunt Rose put a tired hand to her forehead. 'Oh, great day in the morning,' she sighed. 'I forgot about you and Meredith. Yes, they are both coming. Well, after all, I'm their godmother, you know. Is Meredith the girl you had that torrid affair with in Spain?'

He looked down at Mandy. He seemed to be studying her huddled shape, wrapped up in the towel, but not really covered. He was turning some scheme over in his mind. She could almost see the gears turning in his head. He came to a decision.

'Maybe you're right, Aunt Rose,' he said softly. 'Maybe the only way we can rescue Amanda's reputation is for us to get married.'

His aunt turned up her nose at him. 'You don't propose to marry this little girl just to get Meredith Clemson off your back, do you? That's despicable!'

'But—dammit—you just got through telling me out of hand that I *had* to marry her. That *is* what you meant, isn't it?'

'Perhaps it isn't as bad as it seems. Tell me your ridiculous explanation for all of this.'

'Believe me,' he sighed, 'you wouldn't believe me. If I swore to it on a ten-foot stack of Bibles, you wouldn't believe it. Let it go, Aunt. You caught us red-handed.'

'In that case,' his aunt returned, 'there's no doubt in my mind that you'll have to marry the girl.'

'Perhaps we're a step too forward,' Brian commented. 'You and I agree. Do you suppose we should consult Amanda?' He walked over to the edge of the bed, knelt down to be at eye-level with her, and said, 'Amanda Small, will you marry me?'

Her mouth had been hanging open all this time. She closed it with a snap. They've been talking about me as if I were a dressmaker's dummy, she told herself. And all for what? There's a perfectly good and acceptable reason why I was standing here nude in Brian's bedroom. Perfectly reasonable. Only—here I am poised on the edge of another precipice, and he can't understand me. How can I explain it all? I love him—I think. The only thing I really want in all this world is to marry him—and I can't tell him why! If I agree—then what? Look at him scowl. He is obviously proposing to keep out of the hands of some predatory woman. He sees me as the lesser of two evils. And if I accept, without explaining why, won't I be as bad as he?

She shrugged her shoulders. Heads or tails? her conscience nagged. He'd asked her to marry him. All for the wrong reasons, but an offer nevertheless. And in front of witnesses!

That part brought on the silent giggles that shook her body. Liza got up off the floor, put her front paws on the bed, and licked Mandy's nose. Three votes out of four, she told herself, laughing. Oh, what the hell? Sweet, biddable Amanda. I'll give him biddable!

She pushed the dog aside and looked deep into Brian's eyes. 'Yes,' she signed. 'I love you.'

'You don't have to thank me,' he said, 'but I do think we should seal the bargain with a kiss.'

'A diamond ring would be better,' Aunt Rose snapped. She grabbed Liza by the collar and stalked out of the room, pulling the dog along behind her. The bedroom door slammed behind them. Outside in the hall the old lady wiped a tear from her eye and smiled tenderly at the dog. 'You did a good job, mutt,' she told Liza, 'although why it took three days for me to teach you such a simple trick I'll never know.' She reached into the pocket of her dress and pulled out a liver pellet for a reward.

Inside the room Mandy looked up in some doubt at Brian. Is it right? she asked herself again. Can I love him enough for two? What if he loves Meredith, but isn't sure of it? But he gave her no more time to think.

He pulled her off the bed and on to her feet. She lost her sarong in the process. He pulled her close, lifting her off her feet and gently touching her lips with his. She hesitated only a moment, and then abandoned all pretence to demureness. A spark of desire flashed between them as they clung together. His hard, matted chest crushed her full breasts, his warm hand glided up and down her spine from shoulder to thigh. Her tiny hands clutched at the hair at the nape of his neck, pulling him closer, until she dissolved into him and was happy.

CHAPTER FIVE

IT BECAME clear to Mandy that her wedding was not going to be what she had dreamed. Brian brought up the subject after dinner on Friday night. Aunt Rose, Mrs Duggan, Mr Rutherford, and Liza were all present for the discussion. Most of it went right over Mandy's head. It wasn't that she found the subject uninteresting. But she had to get her priorities right, and there he was, sitting by the fireplace in the cool of evening, looking every inch the sovereign of all he surveyed. And the thing he was surveying the most was Amanda Small. She returned the compliment, unconsciously licking her lips as she examined him from keel to top-mast. The conversation flowed around and over both of them, but never sank in.

'Well?' Aunt Rose repeated.

They were all staring at Mandy. She looked at Brian, who was shrugging his shoulders.

'The wedding gown,' Rose said firmly. 'Would you like to try on a wedding gown? Handmade in County Clare, trimmed with lace from the Convent of the Good Shepherd at Clonkelly. Used only once.'

It sounded like interrogation time at the local gaol. Mandy smiled apologetically at them all, got up, and walked over to the large blackboard that had appeared out of a blue sky on Thursday.

It seems to be going on all over the house, she thought. *Somebody* is interested in Amanda Small's communication problems. I *hope* it's Brian!

There were three large boards, one each in the kitchen, the dining-room, and here. And three portable ones outside, near the garden, the swimming-pool, and the patio. It restored her confidence no end. She picked up a chalk, pointed a finger at Aunt Rose, and scribbled 'yes' on the board. There was a smatter of applause.

'Thank the lord we've got one point settled,' Rose said primly. 'Now, for the rest. How many bridesmaids?'

It required some thought. Mandy knew a good many women her own age, but in a business sense rather than personal. Still, they can't shoot a girl for trying, she told herself. 'Six,' she wrote.

'Oh, boy!' Mrs Duggan sounded as if she had just discovered a stale fish in the food delivery.

'Flower girls?' Aunt Rose was beginning to be a nag.

'Two,' Mandy wrote.

'Now, take a quick count of the guests.' Mandy looked back at Rose with a blank expression on her face. Number of guests? Outside of me who do I want at my wedding? Not a single name came to mind. Brian tried to be helpful.

'Mrs Purcell?' he volunteered. She glared at him, then made a very straggly mark on the board for one. It bothered her. She looked over her shoulder and saw he was laughing. The look she threw at him would have killed ten ordinary men. With one wild slash of the eraser she removed Mrs Purcell from consideration. Aunt Rose groaned. Mandy reconsidered. There was Dr Hinson—and his wife. She pondered for a minute, then wrote down four, just for luck.

'This is ridiculous!' Aunt Rose got up and paced the room. 'At the very least I can see two hundred!' Amanda's jaw dropped in astonishment. She rubbed out the four and substituted two hundred, with a large question mark after it.

Mrs Duggan nodded agreeably. Aunt Rose looked determined. Mr Rutherford found something in his pocket that required his immediate attention, and Brian cleared his throat.

'How long would it take to set up a wedding that size?' he asked.

'About three months ought to do it,' his aunt replied. 'Guest lists, invitations, gifts, announcements, pre-wedding parties, and beds for all those who come from out of town. Yes, about three months ought to see it done nicely.'

'Be a mite expensive,' Caleb said gloomily.

'Himself doesn't need to worry about the money,' Mrs Duggan contributed.

'Not if we get this damn book finished,' Brian said. 'We're all liable to end up at the poor farm if we don't get this manuscript out in the mail.'

Everyone turned to stare at Amanda. She stared back angrily. Just as if it's all my fault, she raged to herself. He hasn't even dictated the last four chapters yet, and it's my fault? I must write all this down somewhere. When he gets good at the signs I'm really going to give him what-for! Look at them. They're all sitting around thinking of a big wedding. Something out of this world, with all the trimmings, and lots of pictures to show our grandchildren.

The thought triggered off a blush of massive proportions. In order to have grandchildren you first required children. And in order to have children, you— her hands twitched at the seams of her yellow sun-dress. First you had to get married, that was what. What should 'sweet, biddable' Amanda say to all that? Three months to wait?

What sweet, biddable Amanda ought to do, her inner voice insisted, is to pass the buck. Let *him* make the hard decisions. That ought to swell his ego a bit! She walked over in front of Brian's chair, and pulled him to his feet. Perhaps there was some message in his eyes? She looked. There was a message, as plain as a pikestaff. 'All the better to eat you with,' his eyes were saying. She shuddered deliciously, and threw him to the wolves. 'We must do what Brian wants,' she wrote on the board.

'Why, you little——!' he muttered in her ear as he leaned over and kissed her on the forehead.

'The first consideration,' he said, 'is that we want to get married as soon as possible.' She smiled agreement, and managed to insinuate herself under his arm. Of all the things that had been said so far, this was the only one that made sense.

'How soon?' she wrote.

'How about next Tuesday?' he suggested. 'That sounds like a nice well-rounded day.' Mandy dropped her chalk and threw both arms around his neck, kissing him very thoroughly. It felt altogether satisfactory. And it was the first time she had ever initiated a kiss with any man in all her life.

'I take it you agree?' She nodded. 'Then in that case it will have to be a very simple wedding, right?' Her smile faded slightly, and her nod of acquiescence was just a tiny bit hesitant. 'And I'm afraid that after the wedding—immediately after the wedding—we'll have to get back here to finish that book.' Her smile had become a definite loser. 'And we'll have our honeymoon after we finish the book and become solvent?' There was a considerable wait for her third, very tentative nod. It was very hard to smile, she discovered, when only one eye was co-operating. The other one was trying very hard to cry. But she managed.

If authors didn't have a great deal of money, certainly they had to have a great deal of credit. Or so it seemed. Brian proposed on Thursday night, the wedding plans were mapped out on Friday night, and on Saturday she awoke a little late.

Both Liza and Brian were sitting by her bed, waiting for her to stir. Her hair was a mess, and she had a bad taste in her mouth. But she mustered up all her aplomb, gravely sat up in bed, and smiled at them both. He was carrying a small jeweller's box in his hand. The lid was open, displaying a platinum ring with a beautifully cut diamond enshrined on it, flanked by sparkling diamond chips.

There was no need to call on her acting ability. She was overwhelmed. He kissed her palm, then slipped the ring on the proper finger. There were a few nice things said, she smiled again, he squeezed her hand gently, and went downstairs.

But with that problem aside, teeth brushed, hair combed, she was prepared to admire and be admired. She dressed slowly, waving her left hand needlessly in the air to catch the sparkle. All of which prolonged the dressing—until she smelled smoke!

The smell was augmented by a large amount of conversation from below, mostly in Brian's deep voice. Mandy took one last look in the mirror and hurried downstairs, prepared to be a peacemaker. Brian and his aunt were confronting each other in the kitchen, under a cloud of black smoke that was rising from a large frying-pan.

'Well, you knew Mrs Duggan has weekends off!' He was trying to defend himself in a losing cause.

'But you didn't tell me that you couldn't boil a pan of water,' his aunt pointed out in a very cool voice.

'You're the one to talk. How could you, a fine figure of a woman, live to be sixty-five and not know how to fry an egg? Is that reasonable?'

'Yes, it is, and it's because of that that I'm a fine figure of a woman!' His aunt paused to preen. Even in a long housecoat and slippers, her hair up in curlers, she looked a magnificent lady. 'I've spent my life in *couture* instead of slaving for some man over a hot stove. And I've always made sure I had enough money to hire help for the whole week! Are you broke, or just a cheapskate?'

'Oh, hi, Mandy.' He smiled at her as if he and his aunt were exchanging pleasantries. And maybe they are, the girl told herself. This is one nutty family! 'Sit down at the table,' he added. 'We're getting breakfast.'

'Not that I can see,' Rose snapped. 'Stand still while I wrap this bandage around your hand. Any idiot who pours a pan of boiling water on himself deserves what he gets. Stop whining, I haven't begun yet.'

'Yeah, but it doesn't hurt *you*. And don't nag. I'm a writer. All I have to know is words and typewriters.'

'Don't give me that!' His aunt was having trouble with the adhesive tape. 'You might know words, but you had to hire this little girl to make the typewriter go, didn't you?' And with that they both plopped themselves down at the table and grinned at each other.

Brian strummed the fingers of his good hand on the table-top. 'So, who's going to make breakfast?' He stared at his aunt. She was busy studying a crack in her finger-nail polish. There was a long pause as they tried to out-wait each other. Cautiously, trying to be unseen, Mandy got up from the table and walked over to the stove.

The two of them were still trying to out-stare each other as she replaced the burnt skillet, whipped up half a dozen eggs, and scrambled them, adding a touch of cheese to the mix as it coagulated. In between times she popped bread into the toaster, moved a couple of plates over to the stove-top to warm, and, when the eggs were ready, filled both plates. A moment later the toast popped, and she plonked a full dish in front of each of the Stones. They stopped staring at each other and stared at her. But only for a moment. The food attracted them.

'Nothing makes me hungrier than a good fight,' Aunt Rose declared between forkloads.

Mandy stepped back from the table, hands behind her back, ready to accept whatever accolade might be going around at this time of morning. But Brian pushed back his plate, looked over at her with a mournful face, and said, 'I can't eat this.'

Lord, what have I done wrong? she asked herself frantically. What can go wrong with scrambled eggs? 'Why?' she signed hesitantly, almost afraid to find out.

'Because I don't have a fork or a spoon,' he chuckled. His aunt almost choked over the last bit of her egg, and managed to rescue herself with a sip of coffee. Amanda stood, thunderstruck, and stared at him. 'I don't have a fork or a spoon.' And a big grin! Funny! I rescue them both from blood-letting, and he makes ten-cent jokes. I don't have a fork, indeed! She glared at him, struggling to keep control of her temper. I must have been wrong, Mandy told herself. Who could be in love—really in love—with such an oaf as that?

He pushed his chair slightly away from the table, reading the rage in her eyes. His aunt sat back too, and chuckled. 'Nothing like a good fight to clear the air,'

Rose commented. Mandy added *her* to the list, shooting her a glare cold enough to freeze Hawaii.

Very stiffly, counting backward from one hundred as she went, Mandy stalked over to the utensil drawer, picked up a fork and spoon, and thumped them down on the table beside his plate. 'Thank you,' he offered, trying to ignore the chill in the room. 'I'll have some more eggs after this, please!'

'You are an adventurer,' his aunt chuckled. 'A real daredevil! Look in the girl's eyes, you fool!'

Darned if you won't, Mandy thought as she stared at her future husband. Darned if you won't! She went back to the skillet and spooned out the remaining cooled eggs on to a separate plate. As she turned around, plate held high in both hands, he grinned at her. Aunt Rose, who was good at reading body language, scraped her chair back from the table and tried to get out of the way. The loaded plate hovered just directly over his head. Mandy's hands were trembling, driven by the urge to dump the whole thing on top of him. He sat very still, fork frozen in his left hand, eyes straight ahead. She struggled with her devils and the plate rocked back and forth. Sweet, biddable Amanda, she thought. And I *do* love him. I'll biddable him, and teach him a real lesson. I'll—I'll marry him on Tuesday! I must keep saying that, though. I *do* love him. I *do*.

Gradually she regained control, and gently lowered the plate to the table. He flinched as it went by his shoulders. The plate dropped the last half-inch with a thud. She stepped back, scrubbing her hands as if dry-washing them, and then stomped out of the kitchen on to the patio. As the door closed behind her stiff, un-yielding shoulders his aunt said solemnly, 'That's just what you need, Brian, a nice, sweet, biddable girl!' Her laugh followed Mandy all the way out to the garden.

And so, at ten o'clock on Tuesday morning they were married in the white wooden Congregational Church in the village, with all the villagers who could spare the time—which meant everyone except the shellfish warden—in attendance. The Irish wedding gown was a perfect fit, designed in the Edwardian style, with high choker collar, lace bodice, and a short white train. But no veil. Brian looked even more huge, even more distinguished, as he waited for her at the altar, dressed in morning clothes.

She walked down the aisle on Mr Rutherford's arm, with Becky as her only bridesmaid. There was only one moment of hesitation. Just at the point when she was about four steps from the altar rail, she recalled the dream that had haunted her for so long. Suppose he were not Brian? She shuddered needlessly as she took another step, and he turned towards her. It was the same warm, smiling face, the man for whom she had waited all these twenty-one years. And when Mr Rutherford gave her hand into Brian's, she felt that she had finally come home.

They came out of the church to the thunder of the organ, into a bright summer sun. Amanda Small had disappeared, and Amanda Stone had become the new mistress of Fernald Farm. She tried the name out a couple of times as they stood in the porch of the church, waiting for the photographer to do his work. 'Mrs Amanda Stone.' No, that didn't quite have the ring to it. Mrs Brian Stone! It jingled quite nicely.

She would have loved to run over to the big oak tree in the church yard and carve their initials on it. It was something that Amanda Small would have done. But

Amanda *Stone* was an entirely different sort of person—
at least she *meant* to be—and however the devil long it
took, living with this outrageously wonderful man, she
would restrain her temper, mend all her evil ways, and—
it was too much to expect. She clutched at his arm and
giggled wildly to herself. And the tree was preserved.

Their wedding reception was held at the farm that
afternoon. The place was packed with Brian's family
friends who came to sample the champagne and to toast
the couple. They were all strangers to Mandy. She clung
close to her husband, keeping a hand on his arm. He
introduced her to all and sundry, and occasionally
squeezed her hand. She drank five glasses of champagne, which were four more than she had ever drunk
in her life, and when the last guest disappeared, around
nine o'clock, the bride was just the tiniest bit looped.

The family gathered for one last toast in the quiet of
the study after the last guest had roared down the
driveway. A fire was lit. Mandy had indicated casually
in Mrs Duggan's presence that she loved to watch the
flames. But the July temperature was over eighty degrees
outside, just an hour after sundown. Aunt Rose devised
a compromise. She put two more logs on the fire, closed
all the windows and doors, and turned on the air-
conditioners. Mandy, from her strategic position on the
edge of the divan, shook her woozy head at the crazy
logic of the Stone family, and belatedly remembered that
she was a Stone too. Rose finished off her glass, made
some inane remark about 'early to bed,' and disappeared. Which left Mandy alone in the night—with her
husband.

She gulped the last of the sixth glass of champagne,
wondering why she was having so much trouble focusing
her eyes. She curled her legs up underneath her on the

divan, and stared at him. He sat quietly in the lounge chair opposite, occasionally poking at the fire. If he's waiting for *me* to do something, she cried to herself, I don't know what it is! She pleaded with her big eyes for some sort of guidance, but he made no response.

It must be time for us to go upstairs, she thought, and we'll—and I don't know how! She stood up and paced in a wobbly line back and forth in front of him. It took a minute to build up her courage, to ask the question. She picked up a pad from the table. 'Tell me what to do,' she wrote. He looked at the pad, at her, and a wide grin covered his face.

He chuckled. 'Sweetheart, you're soused. Filled up to the earlobes with champagne. Struggle upstairs and go to bed. I'll be along in a little while.'

Her tensions immediately eased. He had taken charge. She relaxed enough to smile at him. He was mistaken about her drinking, of course. Mr Rutherford had advised her. 'Stick to the champagne,' the old man had said. 'You only get drunk when you mix your drinks.' And so she had taken nothing but champagne since two o'clock in the afternoon. But it did give her a little glow to realise that Brian was only human, and could miss a matake—make a mistake—just like everyone else. And obviously *he* knew what to do on their wedding night, so everything was bound to turn out all right. She floated up the stairs some six inches above the risers, and wandered into her—into their bedroom, where she plumped down on the king-sized bed and giggled.

Someone had laid out her new nightgown. A silk classic, the one with the V-neck that stretched all the way down to her navel. She hung up her wedding finery carefully, showered, and dried her hair. It took a great deal of doing.

Getting into the nightgown proved almost impossible. Its silky smoothness kept slipping through her hands. With a great deal of patience she finally managed it. She didn't tie the bows, or button the buttons. At least she knew *that* much about honeymoons. Walking around the bed was like running an obstacle course. The rug seemed to be wrinkled—she stumbled several times. That's something to be seen to in the morning, she told herself solemnly. Mistress Stone, get your rugs straight!

The bed welcomed her as she slid in gently, trying not to ruffle her fragile gown. Her hand automatically went to the light switch, but a second in the darkness frightened her. Not that she had a fear of darkness, but this was a new time, a new experience, and if he could not see her she could not communicate with him. It was a dark challenge that lurked in a tiny corner of her mind, always ready to pop out. How could he want a woman like me? But then, through the mists that fogged her mind, came another thought. This is our wedding night. Surely he won't want to *talk*?

She closed her eyes for just a moment, to rest them, and as the town clock struck eleven she fell asleep. Some time later she had the tentative feeling that someone had come and gently pressed warm lips to her cheek, but it was too hard to separate the real world from the dream world, and she was tired.

She was awakened at five o'clock on Wednesday by the sound of running water. The bed next to her was empty. He's in the shower, she told herself. But one eye forced open with much difficulty discovered rain drumming at the window in the pre-dawn glow. Weary and disappointed, she fell asleep again, into a dream fashioned from the desires of her heart. In her dream he came to her, still damp from the shower. He pushed

Liza off the rug beside the bed, and slid between the sheets. She turned to him in her dream, resting her cheek on his chest. His arms wrapped around her, holding her safe and close. And she dreamed that, comforted, she fell asleep in his arms.

It was nine o'clock when she opened her eyes again, and this time it was no dream. He was really there, half sitting in bed, with her head resting on his lap. She squeezed both eyes closed, afraid to move. He twisted little tendrils of her hair into backward curls, and ran his fingers along the smooth curve of her cheek. She looked up at him and smiled. He smiled back.

'Party's over, Cinderella,' he chuckled. 'Back to the hearth and the ashes. Hop to it, Mrs Stone. I've left you five tapes in the office, and we have a deadline to meet!' He threw the covers off both of them and gave her a gentle pat on her bottom. On her naked bottom. And he was naked too! He bounced out of bed, stretched, and picked up his robe. She watched the play of light across the fluid muscles of his chest, the ridged muscles of his shoulders. He shrugged his way into a robe. 'Come on,' he coaxed, and whacked her bottom again, a little harder.

It stung. She looked a reproach at him, but he only laughed as he walked out the door. She sat up in bed and rubbed her forehead. It was hard to discriminate between dream and reality. What had really happened during the night? Had he come to her in the darkness, and taken her? Without waking her up? It hardly seemed possible, but then she was no judge of possibilities. How could she know without asking him? And that would require more courage than—Mrs Stone—could muster this day. It's the second day of my real life, she told herself, and hugged the secret gleefully to her.

She breakfasted on coffee and toast, ignoring the plate of ham and eggs which Mrs Duggan sat in front of her. Nothing was said. Evidently a bride was expected to have an upset stomach, she thought, even though I haven't anything to be upset about—have I? She pushed away from the table and went over to the workroom.

He was already in his favourite writing position, lying flat on his back on the divan, talking into the microphone. He looked up as she came in, and turned off his recorder. Timidly she signed to him, 'I love you.'

'Yes, I know you do,' he returned. Her startled expression seemed to amuse him. 'I bought a book. We'll do our practice after lunch. There are a bunch of tapes waiting, and we have one hell of a deadline, so get cracking, lady.'

She struggled slowly over to the typing table, and then changed her mind. Her feet carried her back to the divan. She leaned over and kissed him gently on the forehead. He continued his dictation without a pause. Love me, love me, she prayed. He didn't get the message. She shrugged her shoulders and went to the typewriter. The tapes were stacked chin-deep. It was obvious what he had been doing most of the night. She felt a sharp pain just under her heart. Could one be jealous of a dictation tape?

Disgusted with herself, she slammed paper into the machine, clamped the headset over her ears, and began to fill up the paper at top speed. By noon she had finished chapters fifteen and sixteen. She stacked the pages in neat piles, put them in manila folders, and dropped them on the desk.

He stopped talking into his machine, came over, and spot-checked a few pages. 'Perfect as usual,' he called.

She sat at the typewriter with her hands folded. Perfect as usual? If I were all that perfect, we'd still be upstairs in bed. What have I done wrong? I've had twenty-one years to learn how to be a woman, and obviously I've failed. But then, he's never said he loved me. And not once has he said a word about my—about my voice. Handicap, she had been about to think—but that was a word she hated with a passion. I'm *not* handicapped, I'm just—different! She sat quietly, dejected, feeling rejected.

'Lunchtime,' he called over her shoulder.

She followed him out to the kitchen, dragging her heels. Something had happened to Mrs Duggan's fine cooking. The soup tasted like dishwater, and the sandwiches were made out of cardboard. Nobody else seemed to notice. Mr Rutherford shared the table without a word. As he got up, evidently perfectly satisfied with the horrible meal, he tapped her on the shoulder. 'Some days is better than others,' he said, and walked out into the rain. She wondered dismally what the devil he was talking about.

She and Brian were back in the workroom within the hour. She had interspersed sign-language instruction between bites of the luncheon sandwich. There was no doubt about it, he was a learning whiz. He was mastering in days what had taken her months to absorb! But then she had been a child. He put his arm around her waist as they walked down the hall. That, and his rapid learning, gave her a small lift—just a tiny one. Lord, how easily I'm satisfied these days, she thought. He's giving me crumbs, and I'm acting as if they were whole loaves! When she ripped the cover from her typewriter it split down the middle. She threw it to the floor and stomped on it, but her husband had his back to her.

The afternoon tapes dealt with the interwoven love-story. He was a good wordsmith. The scenes were real, the emotions deep, and Mandy had trouble separating her own reality from the picture he was painting. As the story unwound through her fingers, she was winding herself up tighter and tighter. If only he would say to her what the hero said. If only she could say to him—daydreamer! The little hard ball of depression in her stomach was growing by leaps and bounds. As the depression grew, so did her anger. She had the mad urge to stand up and throw the typewriter at him. She called a halt, and as her fingers coasted to a stop she looked at him. He was no longer dictating, but sitting at the desk with a pencil in his hand, evidently laying out the next sequence. She mouthed several unprintable words at the back of his head, but he was impervious to it all. And why not? she sighed. He was impervious to me in my bed—why should it be any different down here? She bent to the work again, and suddenly it was six o'clock, and she was feeling very sorry for herself. Brian had disappeared, and the rest of the house was quiet.

She shut off the machine, tried to cover it with the torn canvas, then wadded the cover up and threw it into the fireplace. Counting to ten didn't help. She tried counting to fifty. Several times. Then she sat still, hands in her lap. The house had a hollow, empty sound to it. Only the fitful clatter of the rain on the window-pane kept her company. Restless, a tear leaking out of one eye, she got up and paced the room. A decanter of his favourite brandy sat on the shelf. They say it's good for what ails you, she sighed. And why not, Mrs Stone? Nobody else seems to give a darn about you!

She filled one of the wine glasses that stood on the adjacent shelf to the brim. The glass went down in three massive gulps. It burned like fire, searing her throat and stomach. A hasty slug of water from the nearby carafe put out the fire. She still felt miserable. One glass was just not going to do it. She refilled, and toasted herself. Here's looking at *you*, she told herself, and tossed the second one down. It burned, but not so fiercely. Here's looking at *you*! Why couldn't I have married Humphrey Bogart? she moaned soundlessly, and tried to comfort herself. Not with more brandy, she told herself. Try a little logic.

You know what your problem is, Amanda, she lectured. You expect immediate results from everything. You have to allow for initial disappointments. Who knows what he's doing? He's a big boy, who married you to fend off some other female! That thought was too much to bear. She jumped to her feet and paced the room. Once, twice, three times, beating the palm of one hand with the other fist until both were tender. The walls of the room seemed suddenly confining, as if she were locked in a cell whose walls threatened to squeeze her to death.

Her only refuge was the porch. She marched to the french windows, managed to open one panel, and stepped out into the fresh air. There was more pacing room available. She paced. Up and down, with the gradually rising wind playing in her hair. A hunting owl diverted her for a moment, but only for that. Her anger was mounting, like the build-up within a volcano. Lucky he's not here, she told herself. I'd murder him dead!

Amanda Stone, who cried only at catastrophes, had found one worthy of her tears. He married me to fend off Meredith Clemson, she mumbled silently to herself— and to keep his typewriter warm. And what I really want to do is to keep his bed warm!

She moaned in disgust at the terrible mess she had made of her life. The moan came rattling down her throat like a hoarse whisper. She had known all along that she was not beautiful, but surely there was enough to make him want her? Surely there was! In her mind she recalled her tall, stately mother, a Greek statue come to life. Oh, Mommy, she cried to herself, like the little girl she had been, why couldn't I have looked like you? Still crying, she struggled upstairs and fell asleep on top of the covers. Again he had not come.

CHAPTER SIX

MANDY woke up the next morning to a bright sun, and the biggest headache in the world. She didn't remember undressing, but obviously she had. She was in her sprigged minigown, and yesterday's clothing was folded neatly on a chair. And somehow she was in bed, when she distinctly remembered falling asleep on top of the covers. Except for herself and Liza, the room was empty. She stumbled out of bed, careful not to jar her wounded head, and sat down cross-legged on the rug. The big dog moved closer, laying its head in her lap. She fondled the soft ears and scratched gently along the curve of the throat. The dog made agreeable noises and licked her hand. She took a deep breath. The third day of my marriage, she told herself, and here I am making love to my dog. Sadly she pushed Liza away, struggled through her ablutions, swallowed two Tylenol tablets, and went downstairs to face the day.

Mrs Duggan had definitely lost her cool hand as a cook. Breakfast tasted worse than lunch the previous day. The egg resembled an old shingle and the toast like flavoured wrapping paper. She nibbled a bit of each, slugged down two cups of coffee, and walked over to the workroom. Brian was in his usual position, stretched out on the divan. He signed her a 'Good morning.'

She returned, 'I love you,' and went to work.

The love interest in his story was running wild. As she typed she felt a resentment building up. A woman married for three days ought to know all about love. So

either the story was a tissue of lies, or her life with Brian
was a lie!

She just couldn't accept that, and thrust it from her
mind. So deep was she in the story that she hardly noticed when he stopped dictating and began to wander
the room. The empty wine glass, still smelling of brandy,
was on the table. He set it back on the shelf beside the
bottle. He checked the liquid level in the bottle and shook
his head as he moved to where he could see her face.
There was an ink smudge on the end of her nose, and
her hair was in rebellion. He wanted to wipe the smudge
away, to run his hand through her hair, but the work
had to be finished. There was a tremendous gap in the
publication schedule, and he had promised his editor
faithfully to fill it.

Lunch was too much to be borne. Even Mandy's af-
fection for Mrs Duggan could not excuse the unpalatable mess in front of her. Strangely enough, Aunt Rose,
sitting across the table from her, was smiling as she ate
the same stuff, and asked for seconds. Mandy skipped
the sign-language lessons by simply ignoring Brian when
she went back to work, but her heart was not in it. After
a moment or two of fumbling, she took off the headset
and wheeled her chair around to look at him. He was
lying on the sofa, eyes closed, dreaming his way through
another chapter. And paying his lawfully wedded wife
not a nickel's worth of attention, she told herself.

Sweet, biddable Amanda had become too heavy a dis-
guise for her to carry. Rage triumphed over meekness,
and the real Amanda Stone reared her head. Unplugging
the headset, she carefully wrapped the cord around the
headpiece, stood up, and with her best major league pitch
hurled the whole thing into the fireplace. Her aim was
distorted by her anger. Instead of hitting the fireplace,

she bounced the instrument off the two porcelain vases on the mantelpiece. They all fell to the floor together in a rousing crash. Which managed to get his attention.

He was at her side in a second. 'What's the matter, Mandy? Headache?' He *sounded* solicitous, but Mandy was beyond the point where she might offer him the benefit of the doubt. She glared up at him, snatched up her ball-point pen and a filing card, printed something, and pinned the card to the pocket of her very sensible blouse.

'On strike?' Brian Stone was rattled, for the first time in their brief acquaintance. 'Amanda? You can't do that!'

Her pen raced across paper. 'Just watch me!' She jumped to her feet so quickly that the castors on her chair ran over one of his shoes. He made a one-word comment under his breath, but by that time she was striding haughtily towards the door.

'Amanda,' he called after her anxiously. 'You can't do this. I promised the publisher——'

She turned around, and, with fingers flying, told him just what he and his publisher could do. She was going too fast for him to keep up, luckily, because she was suggesting something both immoral and illegal. And then she fled.

Brian caught up with her at about four o'clock. She was stretched out on a chaise-longue near—but not too near—the apron of the swimming-pool, reading a novel. His usual grin was present, but it looked a little worn on the sides. 'I have to make a trip to Providence,' he said hesitantly. 'I have an appointment with my agent. I'll be back by about eight o'clock. Will you be all right until then?'

She gave him a cold nod. Her anger had by no means dissipated, and yet—I wish *I* were his agent, she thought. There must be *something* that will bring him to me. There has to be!

But nothing came to mind, so she returned to the novel until six o'clock. When Mrs Duggan offered a light supper she refused, and went upstairs to her room, brushing by Aunt Rose on the stairs without a word of greeting. She threw herself down on the bed, boiling. The theme of the story she had been typing that morning had upset her. What Brian wrote and what Brian did were two completely different things, and she just could not understand.

Married three days, and I'm still a virgin, she gloomed. What in the world is the matter with me? Am I that ugly? Or has he gotten over the initial entertainment of having a girl who can't talk back?

Or maybe it's just the wrong approach. What I need to do is seduce him! She struggled up from the bed. It was seven-thirty, and twilight was setting in. He would be home by eight, he'd said. She ducked into the shower, then rummaged through her clothes for the sexiest nightgown she could find. It came down over her head like a silken cloud, a substance composed of nothing. The perfume on her wrists and breasts might have been overdoing it the slightest bit. She shrugged her shoulders. As the clock struck eight she was brushing hard at her cap of curls, to keep her hands busy.

Eight-thirty, and he had not come. Nine. Nine-thirty, and still he had not come. Ten o'clock. It's all a lie, she screamed at herself. Every word he wrote about love— it's all a lie! Her body shook with the harshness of the judgement.

Grim-faced, she tore off the nightgown and stomped on it. From her bureau she pulled out her oldest set of jeans, an old shirt which she had worn for years, and her ragged sweatshirt with the words, 'Property of the Harvard Football Team' printed on the front. She fumbled her way into jeans and shirt, and trailed the sweatshirt behind her as she clumped down the stairs.

A fire had been lit in the study again. Nothing in the house stirred except for the flames. She went back into the workroom and picked up the pile of manuscript pages, all of the last four chapters. All of the love-story. She carried it all with her as she stalked back to the study and stared into the fire.

It's all a lie, she told herself. This whole story. It's all a lie, or Brian doesn't love me! Tears flowed, channelling down her cheeks and splattering on her blouse. Angrily she dumped the pile of manuscript pages on to the fire, and watched the blue-tipped flames lick at three days of work. She hunkered back on her heels and watched it burn. Burn, baby, burn! It's all a lie. It's all a lie, and, heaven help me, Brian doesn't love me either. She stood up, a dejected figure outlined by the fire, her shoulders shrunk, her head bowed. Liza stalked into the room and stood beside her, gazing into the flames.

'What the hell are you doing, Mandy?' Brian roared from the doorway. She shrank further into herself. Brian pushed her aside and tried to snatch some of the pages out of the fire. 'The whole damn manuscript?' he roared. 'What in hell is the matter with you, girl?' He grabbed her by the shoulders and shook her until her head waggled.

'Amanda Stone,' he shouted at her, nose to nose. 'That's the most stupid dumb thing in the world to do.

Dumb! Dumb! Dumb! Do you hear me?' A hard shake accompanied each repetition of the word.

Her mind reeled under the impact of the rage he was projecting at her, and her memory shifted instantly through the years. She was standing on the steps of the school again, and a circle of boys was pinning her down. The words echoed through the empty chambers of her mind. Dumb! Dumb! Dumb! Dummy, dummy, dummy, everybody get the dummy!

She put both hands over her ears to shut out the words, but they were already inside her defences, rattling around in her head like deadly bullets. She gasped at the pain and turned to run. He started to follow. Liza had been watching while he shook her, and growled deep in her throat. The dog could not understand why her favourite two people would be hurting each other. But as the uproar continued Liza slowly made up her mind which side to take. She got up, backed into position between Brian and Mandy, bared her huge fangs, and growled a challenge at him. He took the warning for the danger it was, and stopped.

'Mandy!' he shouted after her. 'What the hell have I said? Mandy, wait——'

But she would not wait. She snatched up her bag and sweatshirt from the hall table and ran out the back door into the black night. Her flight took her up the hill into the apple orchard. In the shelter of the trees she stopped, unable to decide where next to go. Her unguided feet took her back down the hill in a wide circle, avoiding the house, across the main road, and down on to the riverbank. As she stepped off the heavy salt-grass on to the sand of the little beach she felt a wet nose thrusting itself into her palm.

Oh, lord, somebody *does* love me, she thought. She dropped to her knees and hugged the animal. They were alone on the beach, the soft waves of the tidal river their only accompaniment. Where shall I go? But reason was overwhelmed by the words rattling around inside her skull. Dummy, dummy, dummy, everybody get the dummy! The moon, a small sliver on the horizon to the east, set a silver glaze on the water, but could not calm her with its gentle touch.

What to do? What else had she ever done when the world assaulted her, and things unseen tormented her mind? Gone back to the rose garden to hide. She stood up, ignoring the fact that the incoming tide was filling her footsteps in the sand. Come on, Liza, she whispered as she slipped her hand under the great dog's collar. We both have the same problem, don't we? Neither of us can explain our hearts!

She dropped the unwanted sweatshirt on an adjacent rock, and started back up the hill towards the road, walking on the grass all the way. The moonlight caressed the old sweater, hanging on the cold rock. It traced shadows across her footprints, that led down the beach to the edge of the incoming tide, and disappeared.

Her shoes were not made for walking. She had slipped into a pair of well-worn rubber clogs. The old road was covered with small pebbles and rocks, each of which bit at her feet and left bruises. One mile to go to the centre of the village, and one mile further after that. None of the streets were lighted, except for the two blocks of Main Street that made up the village centre. Luckily the moon kept her company.

Her mind was running in circles. There was no logic to be found in her logical mind, only those last hateful words which blocked out everything else. The wind sighed in the tops of the trees that overhung the two-lane country road. Ordinarily she might have been afraid. But not tonight. There was nothing in the world that could overcome the misery that clogged her mind. And besides, Liza was padding resolutely along at her side, as if a late night walk were just the thing.

It was eleven-thirty when she came into the crossroads at the village centre. Lights were on in one or two of the buildings, and she remembered the taxi-stand. She found the place, just before Al Munion decided to close down to get an early start on his fishing trip. She wrote her address on his pad.

'OK,' he said, 'T'ain't much out of my way. You the Small girl, ain't you?' She nodded. It seemed hardly worthwhile to correct him. He opened the back door of his old Buick. 'Mighty late to be about, you bein' a girl and all,' he commented. She shrugged her shoulders and pushed Liza into the cab ahead of her.

It was only a fifteen-minute ride to the house. Mr Munion stopped just outside the gate and opened the car door for her. Mandy looked up at the front of the house, shadowed in the moonlight, and shuddered. It looked deserted. The front lawn needed mowing. The windows glared at her like ten Brian Stones, all waiting with a stick to beat her. She hesitated.

'You'll be all right?' Mr Munion quizzed. 'You want I should stay here till you get in?' She shook her head, and managed a weak 'thank you' smile.

'So I'll do it anyway,' he decided. 'Them fish ain't gonna bite until dawn, nohow.'

Mandy waved a thanks and stumbled up the drive, Liza close behind her. Her fingers shook so much that it took minutes to fit the key in the lock. She stepped inside, turned on the hall lights, and came back out on the stoop. Mr Munion waved at her from his car, jerked the old Buick into gear, and started off on his three-day fishing vacation. Mandy walked back into the house and closed the door behind her, leaning against it for comfort.

Saturday morning, and he still had not come for her. She strolled out to the gazebo, stripped off her blouse and jeans to dry, and then decided to take a quick shower in the waterfall. Refreshed, wearing only her briefs and a towel, she stretched herself out on the cushions. Liza came along to sit beside her.

Me and my dog, she told herself. Partners. She can't speak either, but they all understand her. Am I asking too much out of life? Two bees came winging across the garden just over her nose. She mentally thanked them for their work, and dozed off.

It was the noise that woke her. The noise, and the shadow. Liza stirred at something beyond sight, woofed a couple of times, and trotted towards the back door of the house. And then the shadow came between her and the sun. She struggled to open one sleepy eye.

'Mandy?' The voice was hesitant. 'Mandy!' He vaulted up the two small steps of the gazebo and snatched her up off the pillows, cuddling her against his hard chest. Her eyes were wide open—in astonishment. He was almost crying!

'Oh, lord, Mandy,' he muttered into her hair. 'We've had half the village out looking for you. I've been scared to death. We thought you went into the river. We've been dragging the thing from bank to bank, with the State police, the coast guard, and every friend I could dig up!' He pulled her up to his level, and kissed her most satisfactorily. 'Amanda Stone,' he said solemnly, 'you don't seem to realise how much I love you!'

He kissed her again. The spark was still there, stinging them both into passion. Brian, Brian, her heart cried. She put her arms around his neck, pulled his head down, and kissed him back. He hugged her close, and then set her down.

For the first time she remembered that she was standing in front of him, naked to the waist. She snatched up the wet towel and made a loose sarong out of it. He laughed at her attempts at modesty. 'You're my wife, woman,' he chuckled, 'and Liza will discourage any peeping Toms.' He pulled her close again. She struggled far enough away to free her hands.

'You said you love me?' she signed.

'With all my heart,' he returned. 'Why else would I have married you?'

'I wasn't sure,' she signed. 'I thought that you and Meredith might——'

'There is no me and Meredith,' he said. 'Just me and Amanda. Forget the rest of it. Now, what in the world did I say to make you run away from me?' She looked up into his puzzled face to see if he really meant it. He did.

'Dumb,' she signed. 'You called me dumb!'

'Oh, hell,' he said softly. 'I wasn't thinking. I didn't realise. I've never ever set a guard on my tongue. It isn't the Stone way. I was so mad when I saw the manuscript in the fire that I couldn't think straight. Can you forgive me, love?'

The last word melted her barriers. She jumped up and hung on around his neck, kissing him with wild abandon. In the confusion her towel slipped away. He treasured her in his arms, kissed her gently, and set her down. She grabbed at the towel, intending to fasten it. His hand intervened.

'Waste of time,' he said, and for some reason she didn't blush at all. Sweet, biddable Amanda, she thought. Tell me what to do, husband. That contact of the flesh, lip on lip, her soft breasts dimpled against the strength of him, had sent flames up her spine, and she wanted more.

His antennae were on some other frequency, for he failed to get the message. 'We thought you went into the river,' he repeated. 'That damn Mitchell can't track worth a damn. Couldn't even track his own mother, would you believe that? And all we found were your sweatshirt and your footprints, leading straight down to the water line, one way. If that damn Al Munion hadn't come back early from his fishing trip I would have been ready for the mental hospital by now. He called me up this morning. Allowed as how I ought to be interested in where the Small girl had gone, considering that I'd married her. I could have killed him! I could have strangled him with his own fishing lines. Took a little time to call me, he said. He stopped for breakfast and a shower, and then had to read the paper. I could have killed him. Are you all right, Mandy?'

She smiled at him, and laid a finger across his lips. 'Mr Munion is a good man,' she signed.

'I know that, but I got mad anyway. That's the way we Stones are.' She stared uncomprehendingly at him. The ways of men are surely strange, she told herself. Especially this one.

He sat down on one of the cushions and examined her. Her hair was still wet from her impromptu shower, and her cotton briefs, not quite dry, were transparent. What do I do now, she quizzed herself. And for lack of knowledge she stood still, looking the very picture of Aphrodite.

'And why did you burn the manuscript?' he asked. 'Now we have all that work to do over again!' He glared at her, but there was a smile edging the corners of his mouth. He might have convinced her that he was still angry, had he not broken down, pulled her down beside him on the cushions, and murmured into her crown of curls. 'Oh, Mandy, what a fright you gave me. And if you ever do that again I'll—I don't know what I'll do!' He kissed her hard and long, until Liza woofed an objection, and he set the girl free. 'Damn dog,' he muttered. 'She really does think she's your mother, doesn't she? Now, why did you burn the manuscript?'

Mandy struggled with her thoughts. Sign-language was complete, concise, but by no means equal to the spoken word. And his vocabulary was limited. 'I was afraid,' she signed.

'Afraid of what? Certainly not me?'

The dam broke, and her fears poured out as she snatched up paper and pen. 'I was afraid you didn't love me,' she wrote. 'I was afraid I couldn't tell you. I was afraid you wouldn't understand my limitations. I was afraid of Meredith Clemson. And then—on our wedding night—you didn't come. And that made me more afraid.'

'Hey,' he comforted softly. 'Slow down. I can't read that fast, but I'm working at it. There's a lot I can't know about you, love—but I'm trying to understand. And on our wedding night I did come, and you were soused to the ears!'

'I was not,' she wrote. 'I only drank champagne. Mr Rutherford said—I wasn't drunk, just perhaps a little happy. And I fell asleep. It was—a great strain, our wedding day. But then you didn't come the next night either, did you?'

'I came,' he said quietly. 'Lord, Amanda, you were stretched out there so beautifully, so obviously exhausted, that I didn't dare to waken you. I did manage to get you into your nightgown, and under the covers, and then I went back downstairs, had a cold shower, and dossed down on the living-room sofa. That was one of the worst nights I've ever spent, with you upstairs, and me down!'

'Oh!'

'Is that all you can say? So then what happened?'

'I waited for you. You said eight o'clock. I made— special preparations. You didn't come. It made me mad. I thought, why can't he talk to me the way he writes? Act the way he writes? And you didn't come. I thought the book was a big lie, so I burned it.'

Her husband was wearing a very sober face as her pen raced across the page faster and faster. But he knew what she meant. 'There's more than one sign-language in the world,' he said. He leaned over her and kissed her gently. Her head was whirling. He *did* understand! She floated on a cloud bank so high that her feet would surely never again touch the earth. Show me what it is, this other sign-language, her mind shrieked at him, but his thoughts were on other things.

'I've got a picnic basket in the back of the car,' he said. 'I'll go call off the search and bring the basket out here. You look as if you could use some food in you. Be a good girl. I'll be right back!' He stalked off, all the lovable, massive size of him, and left her leaning against the trellis.

He loves me! He said so! What better proof could a girl want? Unless he's just buttering me up so I'll redo that darn manuscript. *We've* got a lot of work to do? Hah! Be a good girl? Hah! I'm tired of being a good girl. But it takes two to tango. I've been a good girl for twenty-one years. I didn't get married to *continue* to be a good girl! I think I'll—her eyes dropped to her clinging briefs.

That's not nice, she told herself. To greet my husband in a pair of dirty, wet briefs. Now stop that immediately, her prim conscience screamed at her. Do you know what you're doing, Amanda Small? Amanda Stone, she corrected. Amanda Stone. Yes, I know just what I'm doing. Go stick your head in a barrel of cold molasses!

With a very large smile on her face she walked back to the waterfall, and liberally splashed herself in the cold water. Then, because her briefs were now thoroughly soaked, she peeled them off and dropped them over a tea-rose bush near the path. There was still the towel to contend with. He won't want me to stand here with my hair all wet, she reasoned speciously. So she used the towel to scrub at her hair and face and arms, until they were dry. Which made the towel too wet to use again as a cover. She draped it sensibly over the rail of the gazebo to dry, and stood waiting for her husband to return, dressed in a very large and welcoming smile.

He came up the path whistling, swinging the picnic basket at the end of one of his long arms. She folded her arms and wondered what to do next. He was admiring her flowers as he came, switching his eyes from side to side, until he came up the steps of the gazebo. At which time he looked up at her, and she unfolded her arms, stretching them out in his direction. His face registered, in rapid succession, welcome, surprise, astonishment—and—what could that last gleam be? she asked herself.

'Mandy,' he said. His voice was hoarse, his breathing irregular. There was an excitement that drove him. She could feel it swarm up from his body to hers. He vaulted up the stairs, snatching at her as a man did water in the desert. His arms came around her and compelled her to his chest, flattening her breasts against the cotton of his light shirt. His hand wandered down across her naked back, down to her hips, and back up again.

She felt the same drive, the same compulsion. Her fingers struggled with the buttons of his shirt, the zipper of his shorts, her fingernails digging into him, her panting, hot breath doing strange things to him. Help me! her mind screamed at him.

He kicked off his shoes, picked her up, and carried her to the pillow-bed. Somehow, in the act of lowering her to the pillows, the rest of his clothes disappeared. They lay together, flesh to flesh, under the open sky, locked in by the scent of roses and their own screaming passions. Gradually, tenderly, he traced lines of desire across her body, from the tips of her toes to her panting mouth. Everything he touched turned her to squirming fire. She wiggled against him, using her hands to arouse him further. After minutes which seemed hours, he forced one of his legs between her thighs. Gently, knowing her inexperience, he coaxed her to the final summit. And then, exploding in a moment of wonderment, he took her.

She was swept up in the animal flame of him, urging him on, nibbling with sharp teeth at the lobe of his ear, sweeping her hands across his broad back and down to his hips. She felt the short sharpness of pain, and then surrendered helplessly to the pounding spasms of glory that succeeded it. It left them both breathless, clutching at each other as if fearing some earthquake would dislodge them. That was the moment when Liza padded up the stairs, licked his ear, and interposed her cold nose between them.

'Oh, no,' he groaned in a pseudo-groan. 'Just married, and already I have mother-in-law problems!' He rolled off on to his back. Mandy pulled his head closer and nibbled his ear again, and they both laughed. The sort of laughter between two people who knew they lived in a world apart, whose metes and bounds were prescribed only in each other. Liza gave them a disgusted look, and ambled out to inspect the garden.

Mandy pushed herself slightly away from him, and stretched like a satisfied cat. He lay with his hands behind his head, an extremely large grin spread all over his wonderful face. Well, he must have enjoyed some part of it, she told herself primly. She was beginning to come down from her high, and the pillows were scratchy and uncomfortable. Now, why couldn't I feel that before? she asked herself. I wonder if he—I wonder if he could make me forget it all again? What a wonderful thing it is to have a man of your own! I wonder if he could do it all over again? Does he have a 'start' button some place that I could push?

She rolled over on her side, facing him, and began to explore with her cool little hands. She found the button. He turned to her tenderly. Slowly, using a great deal more patience and considerable more excitement, he proceeded to do it all again.

They both napped, resting comfortably side by side, his arm thrown across her body, his hand just under the swell of her breast. Liza woke them up at four o'clock. The telephone was ringing in the house. Brian raised himself on one elbow and looked around, as if surprised to find himself in the garden.

'Hello, Eve,' he said softly, tickling her nose.

She opened one eye, not quite prepared to face the world. 'Eve?' she signed.

'You and I,' he laughed. 'Adam and Eve in the garden. Any serpents hereabouts?'

She found him hard to understand in this mood. She knew his rages, she knew his love, but this light-hearted approach was still beyond her, and she wanted to tread carefully. 'We have some garter snakes down by the brook,' she signed.

'OK,' he chuckled. He stood up, and for the first time she really examined the long, lanky maleness of him. All mine, she congratulated herself. Every bit mine! She sat up, keeping as close to him as possible, not at all embarrassed by their total nudity. That's what he means, she told herself as it all became clear. Adam and Eve, naked in the garden, knowing no shame because it did not exist. But there's a snake somewhere, named Meredith Clemson!

'Hungry?' he asked. She nodded and looked around for the picnic basket. He sat down on one of the wire chairs while she scrambled to her feet. The chair swayed under his weight. She held her breath, expecting catastrophe, but nothing happened. She set the wire table on its spindly legs and began to unpack the feast.

He stretched. The chair groaned. 'Amanda,' he said, 'in the interest of harmony and good appetite, would you kindly cover yourself somewhat? The chicken looks nice, but you look nicer, and I'm not sure I've got the strength.'

'Yes,' she signed. 'Whatever you say.'

'Cut out the hokum,' he returned. 'I'm re-evaluating that bit about wanting a sweet, biddable wife!'

She turned up her nose at him, but took a minute to pick up the towel from the rail and wrap it around her waist. 'I'm not sure that's enough, woman,' he growled at her as he struggled into his shorts. The towel covered her adequately from waist to knee, and she could see nothing wrong with her firm, full breasts—even though they were a little tender from unaccustomed hands.

'Too bad about you,' she signed, adding a disdainful sniff.

'Why, you little imp,' he growled, and made threatening gestures. She dodged around to the other side of the table, and finished emptying the basket.

'One hunger at a time,' she signed to him. 'Eat a chicken leg. It's good for what ails you.'

'I might have known,' he sighed. 'Henpecked already!'

Oh, no, she thought. Not henpecked. That's not the way to start a married life. But it's so darn hard to tell whether he means it or not. Look at the big oaf. He's wearing a mournful face, and a put-upon attitude, but his eyes are sparking at me as if he's laughing inside. Just like my mother—why *did* she laugh like that?

'Apologies,' she signed. 'I did not mean to be bossy.'

'You're forgiven this time.' He waved a chicken leg at her to emphasise his point. 'But don't let it happen again.'

'No, sir,' she signed, and dug into the food.

They walked more quickly up to the house. He had the empty picnic basket in one hand, and kept the other around her waist. He opened the back door and stood aside for her, but she held back, looking down on her pride, her refuge, her garden. Which I will never need again, she told herself. I don't need a refuge. I've got a home to go to. She snapped her fingers to get his attention.

'You must sell the house for me,' she signed. 'The money will be part of my dowry.'

'I don't understand the last word,' he said. She laughed out silently at her garden, blew it a kiss off the tops of her fingers, then led him into the warm kitchen.

'Dowry,' she wrote on the kitchen slate.

'Oh, that,' he laughed. 'You're a little out of date, love. Why should you bring a dowry? Yourself is enough!'

'Because I want to,' she signed ferociously. Because I can never be independent again if I come to you with empty hands! But, of course, that part was something she didn't want him to know.

'All right,' he said, looking at the temper building up in her eyes. 'I'll get to it. We'll put the money in the bank. Anything else?'

'Yes,' she signed, somewhat hesitantly. 'You have to see my lawyers. I want you to arrange it all.'

'Odds and ends, huh?' he said. 'Of course, love. I'll look into it one of these days when I have some time.'

One of these days when I'm away from home, Mandy prayed. She was coming to know this big, proud man better by leaps and bounds. And when he went down to consult with Barton, Brown and Burns she would like to have considerable running room between them for a time!

'So get dressed,' he insisted, pushing her towards the stairs. She ran up them happily, slipped into an old A-line shift which had been overlooked, found another pair of sandals, brushed her hair, and came back down, floating off the tops of the stairs, on top of the world.

He was waiting for her at the foot of the stairs, holding out his arms. At the third step from the bottom she wrinkled her nose at him, and jumped. Ready or not, he caught her, but the impulse sent them both to the floor, laughing. His hand gently touched her chin, and the world exploded between them as her simple dress slipped off her shoulders under the urging of his questing hands.

Liza came over to nose at them, decided it was only puppy play, and walked away with considerable dignity.

CHAPTER SEVEN

MANDY didn't make it down to the kitchen until ten o'clock on Sunday morning. It had been a glorious night. She sighed in retrospect, and stretched all her aching muscles. A girl shouldn't be tired in the morning, she told herself. The ache in her bones said otherwise. Her breasts were tender to the touch. But she was so pleased with herself—and him—that she fairly wiggled over to the stove to start the coffee percolator. His likes were simple. Black coffee, and no conversation until the second cup was empty!

As the pot began to bubble there was a knock on the kitchen door. When she unbolted it, Mr Rutherford came in. He was celebrating the Lord's day by wearing a clean white shirt. Mandy was struck by the thought, and ran over to hug him. His weather-bronzed face turned a little darker, and he cleared his throat nervously.

'Come to fill the swimmin'-pool,' he announced. She gestured towards the table and made drinking motions.

'Don't mind if I do,' he chuckled. 'You kin say lots of things without a word, can't you?'

She smiled happily at him and picked up the kitchen slate. 'Yesterday was the day,' she wrote.

He puzzled that in his mind. 'The day what?'

'That was better than some others,' she scribbled. He cleared his throat again. She kissed him on the forehead, and laughed as his ruddy skin turned even more red.

'What the hell is going on here?' Brian was at the door. 'Are you sitting in my kitchen kissing my wife,

114

Caleb?' Mandy was startled by his anger. She put both hands to her cheeks, hoping that he would not explode. His hair was tousled, and he was unshaven. It was impossible to tell whether his anger was real or feigned. She tried to smooth the situation by pouring his coffee.

'Yup,' said Mr Rutherford. 'Ain't hardly no trouble at all.'

'Well, just don't make a habit of it.' Brian laughed as he accepted the mug of coffee. His left arm surrounded her and held her captive as he sat down.

'Don't take no gettin' used to,' Mr Rutherford observed. 'T'was real nice the first try. Early bird gets the worm—Ben Franklin said that.'

'Amanda,' Brian commanded. 'I'm hungry. Lots of something. No worms!' She stuck out her tongue at him, but started to whip up a western omelette just the same. 'Do I have to sit by the kitchen door at all hours with my shot-gun, Mrs Stone?' he continued.

She nodded, a wicked gleam in her eyes, and dished up his omelette. The kitchen door swung inward, and Aunt Rose sauntered through. She was enveloped in an embroidered Chinese housecoat, with yellow dragons on each shoulder. Mandy shook her head in envy. There was just no possible way that *she* could look that nice, especially in the morning before breakfast.

'I'll have one of those,' Rose said, pointing to Brian's plate. 'Whoever would have thought I would give up my slimming breakfast just so some bride could practise cooking?' Her whole-hearted smile took the sting out of the words. Amanda touched Mr Rutherford's arm and made refill motions.

'Don't mind if I do,' Caleb said, 'If it ain't no problem.'

Amanda turned back to the stove, whistling sound-lessly as her hands flashed through the ingredients. What a glorious day, she thought, skipping back and forth to the table. She stopped to peer out of the window. Heavy clouds were massing over the apple orchard. She shrugged her shoulders. Oh, what a glorious morning, she mouthed. Idiot!

When they had all been served she stood behind Brian's chair, watching him eat, her eyes glued on his face. Her right hand rested possessively on his shoulder. He tilted his head to smile at her, wiped his lips with a napkin, and pulled her down on to his lap. She nestled there, both arms around his neck, and nuzzled at the roughness of his chin.

'Ain't gonna fill no swimmin'-pool this way,' Caleb said as he pushed back his chair.

'Really, Brian,' Aunt Rose complained. 'Can't you save that sort of thing for the privacy of your bedroom?'

'No, I can't,' he returned. 'We have more important things to do in the bedroom.'

'Well, I don't think you need to flaunt it in front of Caleb and me,' his aunt answered in a voice that would have chilled Carnegie Hall.

'Why not? We're got a flaunting licence. Blessed by Church and State, you know.' He kissed Mandy soundly, stood her up on her own two feet, and got up. 'We'll be at the pool, darling. We have to check for leaks and that sort of thing. And the publisher has agreed to a ten-day extension of the deadline.' He and Caleb went out the back door into the garden, and Liza squeezed in.

'Come sit with me for a minute,' Rose requested. She patted the chair that Brian had just vacated. Mandy slipped into it, bringing her own coffee. Aunt Rose sipped, then pulled out a pack of cigarettes and lit one. Mandy declined her offer.

The older woman puffed once or twice, and then ground the cigarette out. 'Children,' she said. 'Do you two plan to have them?'

Mandy wiped the kitchen slate clean. 'He hasn't said,' she wrote.

Aunt Rose shook her head. 'That's the only thing wrong with you, child. You pander to that man. Don't let him treat you like a doormat. A little bit of that satisfies the male ego, but you have to assert yourself. You have to stand up to him!' Mandy almost choked over her coffee.

'Why?' she scribbled on the slate.

'Well!' Aunt Rose was taken aback by the question, and fumbled for a moment. 'Because if you don't stand up to him now you won't be *able* to change him. He's an arrogant man!'

'I don't want to change him,' Mandy wrote. 'I like him the way he is.'

Aunt Rose shook her head in disgust. She lit another cigarette, took two or three puffs, and stubbed it out in her saucer. Mandy shuddered. She hated that sort of mess. Rose returned to the attack. 'And you, do *you* want children?'

'Yes. Four, if possible.'

'Then you'd better start soon. Enjoy them while you're young, that sort of thing.'

Mandy smiled in agreement.

'So you're going to get him to change his mind?'

'No,' she scribbled. 'My mother said that English is a very precise language. Brian told me before the wedding to go down to see Dr Hinson for some pills.'

'Oh, lord,' Aunt Rose sighed. 'Birth-control pills?'

'That's what he said.'

'And?' Rose prodded.

'He told me to get them. I got them. That's all.'

'Maybe that's why I never did get married,' the older woman sighed. 'I never was much for taking orders.'

'Me neither,' Mandy scribbled.

Rose reflected. 'Be careful,' she advised. 'He's a hard man when you cross him.'

Mandy watched her stroll out of the door. There was a great deal of advice in that little sentence. She was walking a tightrope, trying to manage Brian. But I'm not really managing him, she insisted to herself. I'm just—learning to adjust! She danced as she moved from the table to the sink, and twirled as she stacked the dishes in the machine.

Dinner was a long way ahead, and would be typically New England. A buffet of cold meats and a tossed salad. But Mandy felt the need to show off a little on this, their first 'married' weekend. Her selection—an upside-down cake. She was up to her elbows in flour when the front doorbell rang.

The sound startled her. As far as she knew they were expecting nobody, and it was a dreary morning, weatherwise. The bell rang again impatiently. Mandy shrugged her shoulders and rinsed her hands at the sink. There was flour in her hair, on her nose, and on her blouse. She brushed at them ineffectively.

The bell rang again, as if someone was keeping a finger on the button. Mandy wiped her hands on her jeans and ran to the swinging door. Liza huffed, but stayed under the table. The hall floor was highly polished, and Amanda Stone felt very young. She slid the last ten feet, bumping up against the door with both hands extended, laughing soundlessly. The bell rang again. She wiped away the smile, tugged at the collar of her blouse, and opened the door.

An impatient young man brushed her aside, carried two suitcases across the threshold, and dropped them on the floor. He was tall and thin, with smooth black hair and a ridiculous handlebar moustache. His grey three-piece suit was impeccable. He took her to be a servant.

'Edward Clemson,' he announced. 'I've come to drop off my sister. We're a little early, but I'm sure Brian won't mind.'

Mandy looked him over, her hands folded behind her back. It took hardly a minute to decide that he was a most unlikeable man. And she didn't mind at all that he thought her a servant. After all, the servants in *this* house were treated like family! Come to think of it, he just might make a good butler.

A woman was coming up the steps behind him. Mandy gulped. The girl was shorter than her brother, but with his narrow face. Her raven hair dropped down to shoulder-length, with tiny curls set over the ears. Each little hair was meticulously in place. Her face was carefully made up, and her dress a designer's delight. It clung to her over-ripe curves like a second skin.

Mandy managed to get her breathing apparatus working again. Oh, my! And this is the girl that Brian chased all over Europe two years ago? And caught her, I suppose, she thought glumly. A sharp pain stabbed her in the pit of her stomach. It's not fair, she told herself. I need more time alone with Brian. It's just not fair!

'It's the dumb one,' Meredith Clemson said to her brother. 'You remember Aunt Rose wrote about Brian's new sparrow with the broken wing? I've got to make him give up these charitable projects of his.' Meredith walked around Mandy, examining her from every angle, and talking to her brother as if Amanda Stone could neither hear nor talk.

'A babe in arms,' Meredith continued. 'And a homely one, thank the Lord. Look at the mess she's in. It shouldn't take much time to brush her out of here.'

Edward chuckled as he reached over and touched Mandy's chin. She backed away from him. 'I'm sure it won't take you long to clean house,' he told his sister, 'but don't write this one off too easily. She could be a cute little bird if she had enough attention.'

'Don't be silly, dear,' Meredith purred. 'She looks like some sort of tomboy. And obviously she's the kitchen help. My worries were pointless.' She turned to Amanda. 'Well, don't just stand there, girl. Do something! Tell Brian that we're here. Edward has to return to Newport. Bring the luggage. And bring me a cup of coffee in the study.' She stalked off down the hall.

Amanda tried to follow her, but found her path blocked. Edward evidently had more time to spare than his sister thought. He trapped Mandy against the wall by pushing hard up against her in a bear-hug, trapping both her arms at her sides. She sparked anger at him, but with her arms locked in his vice, and her body movements prohibited by his weight, there was practically nothing her karate training could do to help.

She struggled anyway, using her feet to kick out at him. He foiled that by turning his body a half-turn sideways, and resting all his weight on her. Gradually he brought his lips down on hers, probing against the teeth she had clamped shut. Down the hall his sister stood at the study door and laughed.

This one is a strange one, Mandy thought. His kiss was rough. His moustache rubbed a raw spot on her upper lip. He reeked of tobacco. He pressed his lips harder against hers, trying to evoke a reaction. He got it. Utter contempt.

Could it be that Brian is the only man who knows how to kiss me? she asked herself. The thought let her relax. Edward took it for a submission sign, and increased the pressure. He pinned her against the wall, and freed one hand. It began to wander down her side, smoothing her hip, rising towards her breast.

Mandy struggled harder, kicking viciously at him, but missing. The back of her heels drummed against the wall as she swung her feet, echoing her protest down the hall.

The kitchen's swinging door slammed open, banging hard against its stop. Liza came charging out, her paws scrabbling and slipping on the polished floor. Meredith was in the way of the animal's raging charge, and was knocked down for her troubles. Edward failed to hear the dog coming, as his back was turned. Liza caromed into him, knocking both he and Mandy to the floor. She scrambled away from him, huddling herself in the corner. He struggled to his feet. Liza glared at him, taking a position astraddle Mandy's huddled form.

'Call off your damn dog,' Edward shouted in a frightened tone. 'It wasn't meant to be a great rape scene!' He raised an arm in Mandy's general direction. Liza snapped at it, catching the cloth of the jacket in her big teeth, and tearing it half off him. She dropped her grip on the cloth and stalked him. He backed up slowly, keeping his face turned towards the animal. His teeth were chattering. The front door was still open. He backed out and down the stairs. The dog followed him, each step accompanied by a deep, menacing growl. When he bumped into the side of the Mustang he fumbled for the door, fell into the front seat, and slammed the door behind him.

The dog put her front paws on the car window and let her tongue hang out. Edward struggled to raise the window as high as it would go, then climbed over into the driver's seat and tried the starter. It failed to catch. Liza dropped off the near side of the car and went around to the other side, baying at him. He ground the starter again, clashed the gears, spun his rear tyres in the loose gravel, and zoomed away.

The dog took a few steps down the drive to make sure he wasn't coming back, then turned and thumped her way up the stairs to where Mandy still crouched in her corner.

Mandy tugged at the dog's ears and hugged the great head to her breast. Like the Hound of the Baskervilles, she told herself. She had read the book twice, and seen the movie four times. She struggled to her feet, resting her hand comfortably on the dog's head. Amanda Stone and her escort service! The thought tickled her, and relieved the ball of tension that had been hovering in the pit of her stomach. Twice, in this house, she had been attacked and unable to scream. And both times she had been rescued. So there *were* compensations in this adult world!

Meredith Clemson was still sitting on the floor, in a state of shock. Mandy started towards her, wondering if Brian had heard the noise. What would have happened if Brian had come to her rescue, rather than Liza? He had such a terrible temper...

What a day this had been so far. She had kissed two more men. Would Brian appreciate her increasing experience? Somehow she doubted it. Mr Rutherford had been nice. Edward Clemson had been slimy, like kissing a dead fish!

Meredith had struggled to her own feet, and was trying to restore her clothing to perfection. But there was a tremor at the corner of her mouth, which she was trying to hide. She extracted a compact mirror from her bag, and was doing something to her face. That's what I need, Mandy sighed. I need to know something about make-up. I need all the help I can get!

As Mandy approached, the other girl backed slowly into the study. It was the dog, of course, Mandy told herself. Nobody would be afraid of just me. She snapped her fingers at Liza, then gave a command with her index finger. The dog stared at her, as if debating the order, then gradually, in sections, sat down at the door. Mandy followed the other woman into the room.

Meredith inspected the dog carefully, then seemed to find some assurance, and relaxed. 'Edward was only teasing,' she trilled.

Mandy stared at her out of a solemn face. I'll just bet he was teasing. Just like a crocodile teases! Meredith sat down in one of the overstuffed chairs, carefully smoothing her skirts around her. Mandy plopped down into the opposite chair, and they stared at each other.

You're the hostess, Mandy told herself. Do something. She snapped her fingers for attention. 'Coffee?' she mouthed, and made drinking gestures with her hands.

'Yes, bring some coffee. Black. Bring a cup for yourself, too. We can talk together until Brian comes.'

Mandy jumped up and walked out to the kitchen. As she passed Liza, the big dog turned its head to watch. 'Guard,' she signalled. The dog put its head down on the floor, muzzle pointed at Meredith.

In the kitchen there was coffee left in the percolator, but it was cold. Bring a cup for yourself, too. Mandy snorted. The great lady will condescend to drink coffee with the kitchen help! That's funny! Meredith had changed her approach in seconds. The snake has two skins? She wants something. What? Certainly not coffee. She fumbled in one of the cupboards until she found an old jar of instant coffee. The powder was stale, but she made a small pot of it anyway. Mandy hoped she hated instant coffee. Maybe she was allergic to it, and would break out all over her face? That might be nice. In a determined mood, Mandy set up the tray and carried it over to the study.

Meredith was all smiles. 'Sit here.' She pointed to the couch next to her. She raised her voice, too, as if being unable to speak must affect Mandy's ability to hear. And perhaps her brain too. 'I'll pour the coffee, and we'll have a nice talk. You *can* hear me?' Mandy nodded, and offered a vacuous smile. 'And you have some means of communication?'

Mandy pointed to the pad and pencils on the table. Dear Brian. Every room in the house now had a dozen pads and a million pencils! She picked up a pad, squirmed herself comfortably on to the couch and looked up.

Meredith was laughing, a high, shrill titter. 'Poor Brian. Forced to talk to a pencil. He must love that!' Mandy made no answer. 'Well, I mustn't keep you too long from your kitchen duties, my dear. By the way, this is lovely coffee!'

And so much for *your* taste, Mandy thought. She had taken one sip from her own mug, and knew it tasted like dishwater.

'And you can't make a sound?' Meredith probed. Mandy shook her head. The other girl laughed. 'It must be pretty boring around here for Brian. I'll have to do something about that quickly.'

Mandy felt another pain in her stomach. You're not all that sure of Brian, are you? she mocked herself. This woman was determined to turn the knife in the wounds, and Mandy was feeling uncomfortable under that piercing eye.

'Have you been here long?'

Mandy nodded. 'All my life,' she wrote.

'No, I mean in this house.'

Mandy held up five fingers.

'Five months?'

Mandy pulled over the pad and wrote, 'Five weeks.'

'Why, and you're just a child, aren't you? How old are you?'

I'm twenty-one going on ninety-five, Mandy thought, but she held up two fingers on one hand, and one on the other.

'Twenty-one?' Meredith mused. 'Funny. You hardly look sixteen.' Mandy shrugged. What could one say to a statement like that? 'By the way, where is Brian?'

'Filling the swimming-pool,' Mandy wrote.

'Wonderful,' Meredith gurgled. 'I love swimming. I've brought oodles of swimwear with me.'

I'll just bet you have, Mandy thought grimly. And each of them with less material than the one before!

'And some of them are so daring, I wonder that I'll have the nerve to wear them,' Meredith concluded.

I wonder too, Mandy raged, but I'm sure you'll find the nerve. Damn it!

'Do you swim yourself?' The question struck Mandy right between the eyes. She had not thought about

swimming in years. Not since the wild African storm—
the blood dripping down her forehead. She shivered, and
bowed her head.

'No,' she wrote, 'I don't swim.'

'Ah,' Meredith said. The single word was loaded with
meaning. The woman could read facial expressions, and
Mandy was unable to school her face on a subject like
swimming. She was beginning to feel very young, very
inexperienced, very insecure. Brian, her mind screamed,
I need you!

The inquisition went on. 'And you were born in this
area? You must have known Brian for some time?'

Mandy shook her head. 'For five weeks,' she wrote.

'Why, then, you're practically strangers, aren't you?'
Meredith trilled. She must practise that sound a lot,
Mandy thought. It sounds too stupid to be natural. 'Of
course, you realise that Brian and I are old friends,'
Meredith continued. 'He chased me all over Europe,
trying to get me to marry him. It was a case of poor
timing. I wasn't ready for marriage then. Too bad, really.
But now that he's an established author, and I'm a few
years older, I'm ready to settle down. I suspect that he'll
be popping the question pretty soon. I plan to stay four
or five weeks. That should give him time enough, don't
you think?' She was reflecting to herself, rather than
commenting to Mandy. 'I think you should plan to go
home by that time, my dear,' she continued. 'I wouldn't
want you cluttering up the house after Brian and I are
married. You *do* understand?'

Amanda's eyes widened. She bit on her knuckle. A
satisfied expression flashed across Meredith's face. 'You
poor child,' she said, obviously not meaning it. 'I do
believe you've got a crush on Brian yourself, haven't

you?' Mandy nodded. 'That's very naughty of you,' Meredith laughed. 'And now that I'm back you'll have to transfer your attention to someone more in your line. I suppose you think he cares for you too?'

Mandy thought that one over, chewing on the end of her pencil, then printed a large 'Yes' across the page of her pad.

'That's ridiculous.' Meredith leaned closer to her. 'Whatever gave you the idea that Brian cared for such a frimpy little thing like you?'

I wondered myself, Mandy thought. And Brian must have thought a great deal about Meredith. I suppose I'll have to be nice to her, even though it hurts.

'Well?' Meredith demanded. 'What gives you the idea that he cares anything about you?'

Mandy grabbed her pad in a firm hand. 'I think he cares something for me. He married me last Tuesday,' she wrote.

Meredith jumped up from the couch. Her coffee-cup splashed over and fell on to the thick rug. Her face contorted. 'Why, you lying, stupid, dumb little bitch!' she screamed. 'Did you think I'd let you get away with something like that?' She flexed her fingers and extended them, like claws.

Liza got up from her guard-post at the door and walked into the room. Meredith saw the dog out of the corner of her eye and backed away, screaming curses in English and French. Mandy shrugged her shoulders, got up, and walked towards the door, where she snapped her fingers and ordered Liza to follow. She made it to the door just in time. As she stepped into the hall the coffee-tray crashed into the wall just inches away from the door.

Big temper, small aim, Mandy told herself fiercely as she picked up her cake-making where she had left off. I wonder if everybody Brian knows throws things? For another ten minutes she could hear Meredith raging in the study.

CHAPTER EIGHT

MANDY was just putting the cake in the oven when Aunt Rose came in through the outside door. 'I thought I heard a commotion. Is there any trouble?' At that moment there came a crash of glass from the study.

'Trouble,' Mandy scribbled on the slate. 'Miss Meredith Clemson. She is unhappy.'

'Meredith? Oh, my! So what's her problem?'

'She just found out that I am Mrs Brian Stone.'

'Oh, gracious,' Rose fluttered. 'I knew it was all a mistake, bringing them here. But they weren't supposed to come for another week. How could she be here today?'

'Look in the study,' Mandy scribbled.

'I know Meredith has a temper,' Rose said, 'but Edward is usually able to keep her under control. Edward. Her brother. Did he come?'

'Yes.'

'And where is he?'

'He left quickly.' Mandy's hand was tired from writing. She erased the slate and flexed her hand.

'Amanda Stone!' Aunt Rose had a temper of her own, being a Stone born and bred. 'Why did he leave so quickly?'

Mandy sighed. There seemed to be no way to avoid the problem, and, while she didn't mind embroidering the truth on occasion, she was dead set against an outright lie.

'Liza tried to bite him,' she wrote.

'Oh, my! That's not a nice way to welcome people. I wonder what Brian will think of that?'

What indeed? Mandy thought. If he comes and commiserates with me I'll cry. I really will. There was another resounding crash from the study.

'I guess I'll have to see about restoring peace,' Aunt Rose declared. She looked at Mandy again with the same sort of piercing search that Brian used, and then she walked out.

Mandy looked around the kitchen and sighed. There was just too much to clean up after her baking spree. She began. The work was hard, but it kept her mind from thinking too much. I wish I could scream, she thought. I wish I had the nerve to be like all the rest of the Stones and throw things. He'll be furious when he comes in. She's a guest in the house, but that doesn't give her the right to wreck the place.

Brian came in at two o'clock, whistling. He caught her up by the waist, kissed her briefly, and disappeared into the rest of the house. Mandy shook herself, and pulled the cake out of the oven. And she had barely set the pan out to cool when he was back again.

'Mandy,' he said grimly, 'come with me to the dining-room.' She gestured towards the cake on the table. 'Now!' he commanded. She ducked her head, and followed him slowly out into the hall. Meredith was already waiting for them in the dining-room, staring out of the side window. She had heard them come in, but she waited until the last minute, and then acted surprised.

'Oh, there you are, Brian,' she purred. She put her hand on Brian's arm. 'And that naughty child.'

'Amanda,' Brian said, 'Meredith tells me that you set Liza at her and her brother this noontime. She tells me that Liza knocked her down, and bit Edward. Is that true?'

She felt as if the bottom of her world had fallen out. Why me? she yelled at herself. Why is he blaming me? 'Not exactly,' she signed, and her face reflected her mutinous feelings. He shrugged it off sternly.

'Did Liza knock Meredith down?' She nodded. 'Did Liza bite Edward?' She nodded again, and started to sign an explanation. He held up his hand and stopped her.

'There's no use talking further about it. Meredith, will you excuse us, please?'

Meredith patted his arm. 'Don't be too hard on her, Brian. After all, she's only a child.'

'She is not a child,' Brian said coldly. 'And even if she were—well, please excuse us.' The woman nodded and walked out of the dining-room. Mandy could see the very self-satisfied look on her face; Brian could not. There was a strange look in his eyes as he watched Meredith's departure. Tenderness? Love? Mandy cringed at the thought.

'This is inexcusable,' he said. 'You know that Liza and Mitchell are trained attack dogs. They're as dangerous as loaded guns. And to think that one of them would be set to attack our guests—our guests, mind you—is a terrible thing. It must never happen again. And, more than that, I expect you to be polite to our guest—to Aunt Rose's guest, to be exact.'

She tried to explain again, sure that a few words would straighten out the whole mess, but he brushed it aside. 'No!' he said. 'We'll say no more about it. See that it doesn't happen again. You're my wife, not a child, and I expect better things of you!' He turned his back on her and stalked out.

Amanda stood at the window, clenching and un-
clenching her fists. Why, that arrogant, opinionated,
imbecilic, stubborn man! Judge and jury and pros-
ecutor, all in one. I didn't even get to enter a plea! And
that rotten trouble-making overblown hag! I'm supposed to stand here and take it? Go down on my knees
and beg forgiveness, or something? Sweet, biddable
Amanda. Hah!

She stomped out into the kitchen, scowling so sternly
that even Liza struggled to get out of the way. And now
I suppose he thinks I'll run back into the kitchen and
make dinner for him and his lady love! Well, two can
play at that game!

The cake was sitting in the middle of the table, waiting
for its frosting, but it had fallen in the middle. That does
it, she told herself. She picked up the innocent cake,
broke it into three pieces, and threw them out of the
back door on to the patio. Mitchell welcomed the gift
without complaint. Damn the man, she roared silently.
Double damn! The cake plate was near to hand. It scaled
across the kitchen, smashed into the refrigerator, and
splintered into a thousand pieces. The crash made a very
satisfying noise, but it was not enough. She stormed in
circles around the kitchen, picking up anything that came
to hand, and throwing it at the opposite wall.

The war might have continued, but it suddenly struck
her that, the more she threw, the more she would have
to clean up afterwards. It brought her to a halt in the
centre of the room, hands quivering at her sides. That
impossible scraggy man! And his well-travelled, shop-
worn female companion—mistress? Damn! And he
expects a tasty cold plate for dinner? Hah!

Liza did her best to hide behind the refrigerator.
Mandy smiled sarcastically and took revenge on her

husband. She opened the refrigerator and extracted the platter of cold meats over which she had laboured lovingly earlier. The big dog watched cautiously as the entire dinner was set down on the floor. Mandy smiled from ear to ear as the dog lost her manners and made short work of *his* supper. Himself! That ought to teach him a lesson. He could nibble on the tossed salad. She set that out in the middle of the table, and started for the door.

Aunt Rose came in just as Mandy was going out. 'Almost four-thirty,' that worthy lady warned her. 'We don't want to be late with the meal when we have a guest in the house. What's for supper?'

Mandy gestured towards the salad bowl, sitting in solitary splendour on the table. 'That's all? Tossed salad? Meredith doesn't care for salads.'

'Good,' Mandy mouthed.

'Why, you're crying, child. What's the matter?'

She struggled to free a pad from her pocket. 'I am not!' she wrote. 'I'm going to my room.'

'Good idea, love. You have plenty of time to change. I'll set the table.'

'Not for me,' Mandy scribbled. 'I am not going to share food with him ever again!'

'Why—what's the matter?' the aunt stuttered. 'You've lost your cool! Just look at you.'

'I don't want to look at me,' she scribbled.

'I—well—all right, but you have to remember that you're the hostess here, not me. Shall I tell him you have a headache?'

'Tell him my stomach hurts,' she wrote. 'Tell him I've come to my senses and have run away. Tell him——' The point of her pencil snapped. She threw it down, brushed past Aunt Rose and ran up the stairs.

She had no further reserves of strength to draw on. Before she was halfway up the stairs the tears came, full-flowing, unrestrained. The silent sobs shook her frame like a hurricane. Behind her, as she ran, she could hear a wisp of conversation.

'Just what the devil did you do to Amanda?' his aunt demanded. The answer was not clear. Down the hall her legs led her reluctantly to his—their—bedroom. Surrounded by all his things, there was some relief. The tears dried. She pulled out her oldest nightshirt, and snuggled into the huge bed. Her mind whirled. At the first sign of disturbance he had sided with Meredith. She needn't have worried about communicating with him—he hadn't given her a chance. Not a word in her own defence. It had happened, so Meredith must be right!

She boiled in anger, pounding on the pillows with her fist. I'll show him biddable, she promised herself fiercely, and, much to her surprise, fell asleep.

The clink of glasses and an occasional burst of laughter coming up from the open window of the dining-room woke her up. The little clock by her bed registered ten o'clock. She felt curiously refreshed, calm, as she listened. It was Meredith Clemson at her vintage best. Meredith the hunter, stalking. And she's stalking *my* husband! she thought. Like a fool I ran away and left the battlefield all to her. Amanda Stone, you are the biggest, most stupid fool in the world!

She tossed and turned until one o'clock, when she heard his hand on the doorknob. He stomped into the room, slammed his way into the bathroom, and she could hear the shower running. When he came out he was muttering under his breath. The bed swayed as he climbed in beside her. One hand reached out for her. Still boiling in anger, she rolled away from it, landed on the floor, and scrambled for the bedside chair. He sat up in the bed, hands behind his head.

'I take it you're angry with me?'

'Yes,' she signed, with her fingers, her eyes, her facial expression, and her body movements. The whole range. He sighed.

'Amanda,' he said softly, 'you know those dogs are dangerous.'

'I know,' she signed. Her fingers were stiff from the weight of her anger, and had to be disciplined.

'And you don't think I should have reprimanded you?'

'No,' she signed, and glared at him.

'Amanda,' he said patiently. 'I grew up with Edward and Meredith. I've known them all their lives. I have no reason to think that Meredith would lie to me about something like that. Why would you expect me to act otherwise?'

'I'm your wife,' she signed grimly. He reacted like a man who had just locked his keys inside the car. His face paled, and then turned red about the ears. A moment's pause.

'You're right,' he admitted grudgingly. 'I should have thought of that. Explain what happened.'

'No,' she signed. 'You have to trust me. I'm your wife.'

Another long silence as he digested an unpalatable truth. He shifted uneasily in the bed. He sighed gustily. 'I've a lot to learn about being a husband. You're right again, Amanda. What can I say? I apologise with all my heart. You *are* my wife, and I *do* trust you!'

Mandy's pent-up breath rushed out of her in a discernible sigh of relief. He looked startled. It was the first vocal noise he had ever heard her make. 'Then you do forgive me?'

She started to nod, and then stopped. There was more unfinished business. 'The other night,' she signed. 'You promised to be home at eight. You didn't come. Why?'

Her glare was met by a flash of something in his eyes. Devils peered out at her. He waved one hand casually, but the corners of his mouth were twitching, giving away the whole show. 'I'm your husband, Amanda,' he said with a chuckle. 'You have to trust me.'

Hoist by her own petard, she stood frozen in the middle of the floor. His smile expanded into a grin. She fought against the response, but her sense of humour slowly overcame all the anger. It drained out of her, and left her laughing. 'Do you trust me?' he probed.

His vocabulary was too small to understand all she had to say. It's time for Plan B, she told herself. Her fingers fumbled with the buttons of her shirt, and it slowly tumbled to the floor.

She came skipping down the stairs the next morning, as happy as a child. Rose, Brian, Meredith, and Mrs Duggan were all at the breakfast table. She kissed Aunt Rose, signed, 'I love you,' to Brian and even managed a smile for Meredith. They all laughed at her little-girl appearance, accentuated by a demure white-frilled blouse and dark jeans.

'Good morning, love,' Brian said. 'Are you feeling better after last night?' She looked at him with the devil in her eyes.

'Late night or early night?' she signed. He choked on his coffee.

'What in the world are you doing with your fingers?' Meredith asked. 'You know we really missed you last night, so Brian and I had to spend the whole evening in each other's company. And *I* had to make the dinner.'

The purr of satisfaction was recognised all around the table.

And how about that? Mandy groaned to herself. Not only has she a classy chassis, but she can cook too! If I let her get away with more of this she'll cook my goose! Poor put-upon girl. You had to put up with my husband until one o'clock in the morning. But then he came to me! Now there's a compromise we might live with. You can have him all the evenings, and I'll have him all the nights! Her own vehemence made her gasp, and she must have been moving her lips, because Brian was watching her with narrowed eyes. Amanda Stone, she lectured herself, you are becoming a little bitch. Contrilely she came to the table and picked up her slate.

'Meredith,' she wrote, 'I apologise for yesterday.' Her husband caught the message and smiled at her. He pulled her over to him and sat her on his knee, nuzzling at the nape of her neck.

'I understand,' Meredith returned. Her voice was cold, and whatever that look was, it wasn't forgiveness. 'I'm sure it was all too upsetting. But then you are so young, my dear, and with that terrible handicap...' She left the statement hanging in the air and concentrated on Brian. 'Shall we spend the day basking by the pool?' she purred. 'All that travelling yesterday was just too tiring for words.'

'I suppose we could,' he answered, 'but it's a working day for Amanda. You know, last night the bride, this morning the office slave. We had a manuscript almost ready to mail, and some terrible accident happened to it. Mandy has to retype it if we plan to eat next week.'

'For goodness' sake,' Aunt Rose chimed in, 'don't you have anything to wear, child, except those disreputable jeans?'

'Why don't you slip into a bikini and join us at the pool for a few minutes?' Meredith asked. She was trying to sound casual, but the words were strained.

What does she want now? Mandy puzzled. And what's wrong with my jeans? They're clean, perfectly respectable, and only two years old. But watch little Miss Meredith. She knows about me and water. She knows, and she's trying to figure some advantage out of it. What the devil is Brian up to? Meredith is her usually hateful self, Brian acts as if he's got a guilty conscience, and Aunt Rose is on the war-path about my clothes! Heaven help me, are they *all* after my scalp?

But not my Brian, of course. Her heart swelled. I trust him, and he trusts me, and if that's a gleam in his eye it's got nothing to do with scalps. See, I *am* learning something about marriage!

She leaned over to kiss the top of her husband's head, nodded to the others, and went over to the workroom. Brian joined her a few minutes later, bringing her a second cup of coffee.

'I hate to see you work like this,' he said, 'but we do have to meet a deadline.' She nodded warily. Things were not quite as clear to his typist as they were to the great author. 'I think I'll take a few hours off myself.' He was watching her out of the corner of his eye, to judge her reaction. She maintained a solemn face. After all, she told herself, he's got the shovel, so why shouldn't I see how deep a grave he's going to dig for himself?

'I'll try to amuse Meredith and keep her out of your hair. She really bugs you, doesn't she, Mandy?'

She manufactured a sunny smile for his benefit. He assumed it meant an approval. He kissed her gently, and rushed out of the room. There's no fire, love, she yelled silently after him. Take your time. The shark is upstairs sharpening her teeth. But again, he was not on her frequency, and all her smart remarks were wasted.

It took some time for her to sort out all the tapes. She had hardly started when she felt a tap on her shoulder. She removed the headset and swivelled her chair around.

Meredith was standing there, dressed in the skimpiest bikini bottom that Amanda had ever seen. 'I'm having terrible trouble with this bikini top,' she purred. 'Would you mind helping me fasten it? It's so terribly hard,' Meredith continued, leaning forward, 'when you have such a full figure, you know.' How in the world would I know? Mandy asked herself. She's making me feel like a case of stunted growth. For years Mandy had been—well—satisfied, with her 34-21-34 figure. But confronted with Meredith's massive construction she felt like a flat board. There was a noise at the door. Meredith turned in that direction just as Brian came in.

'Oops,' he said, and turned to leave.

'Don't be a prude,' Meredith purred. 'It's only a little problem with a twisted strap. Mandy is helping me with it.' But Mandy could not help but notice how slow the other woman had been in covering her breasts. She jumped up from her typing chair, untwisted the strap and savagely knotted the strings back with a square knot. She tied it tightly, leaving little room for breathing. Then, for good measure, she added another knot on top of the first.

And just you try to get out of that, baby, she mouthed. The game was being so over-played that it was funny. Even Brian looked as if he knew what was going on.

'Well, whatever,' Brian laughed. He looked like Apollo in his swimming-trunks, Mandy thought, and there was a catch in her throat as she devoured him with her eyes. 'Let's get to the pool, Meredith. And you, slave, back to work.' He stood in front of her for a moment, his hand gentle on her shoulder. Mandy snatched up her pad, and just for her husband's eyes she wrote, 'Put your eyeballs back in. They droop, you know.'

'The eyeballs?' he chuckled. Mandy kicked at his ankle and missed. Brian laughed wickedly as he scooped one hand under Meredith's elbow and escorted her out to the pool. His wife leaned on the typewriter for a moment, shaking her head in disgust. It took another five minutes for her to calm down enough to get to work.

She stopped for a noon break. With the window open, and her ears no longer impeded by the headset, she could hear the chatter, and an occasional scream of delight, from the pool. She walked over to the window. Meredith and Brian were lying side by side on an inflatable mattress, and he was tickling the woman. Mandy gritted her teeth, then bit viciously into the ham sandwich which Mrs Duggan brought in. Aunt Rose came along, singing under her breath, holding a plastic tape-measure.

'Stand up straight, dear,' she said. Mandy complied. Rose measured and checked and noted, all the time humming away to herself. She raised a questioning eyebrow.

'Did you ever wonder how a woman can get to be sixty-five and not know a thing about housekeeping?' Rose was in a gay mood, no doubt of that. 'It's because the only thing I've ever been interested in was clothing design. I'm going into the city this afternoon. You can't expect to compete when you dress like a poor relation.'

Mandy shook her head, not comprehending. 'Why do I have to compete with someone?' she wrote.

'Do you want to keep your husband?'

'Of course I do.'

'Then shut up and stand still,' Aunt Rose muttered. She measured and checked one more time. Then, still humming under her breath, she walked out. Mandy watched her go, a whimsical smile on her face. They're all a bunch of fruitcakes, all these Stones, she told herself. And what was that tune Rose was singing? A theme song from some movie—of course, 'Les Girls!' Now what in the devil was she up to?

Mandy shrugged her shoulders. It was something she was doing a lot of lately. Shrugging her shoulders, that was. She went back to work and kept at it for approximately five minutes. The voices out at the swimming-pool had become suspiciously quiet. The stacks of tapes had grown smaller, but not much. *Sweet, biddable Amanda* ripped the paper out of her typewriter, ripped the cover again as she shoved it down on the machine, and stood up. With shoulders aching, she stacked the finished pages, and stretched. What was it Daddy used to say? 'The mind can accomplish only as much as the seat can endure.' Bingo. What the devil is going on out there between *my* husband and that—woman? Well, Simon Legree Stone, this slave has typed her last tape. Amanda Stone is no longer a tape-typer, no matter what happens!

She rubbed her sore flanks, went out to the kitchen to gather Liza up, and the pair went off for their usual walk. They strolled for a good half-hour, through the garden and up the hill until they reached the sharp cliffs that dropped down into the Atlantic. She stretched out on her stomach and peered over. It was an awesome sight. Finally the two of them sauntered back to the house through the pool area. Brian had gone into the house, but Meredith was still stretched out on the air mattress, like some overgrown cat.

'Come for a swim, have you?' the woman asked. Mandy denied the idea by shaking her head.

'You really miss the best of everything. Look how pale your skin is, my dear. Don't you ever sunbathe?' Mandy signalled denial. 'Well, of course, you really wouldn't look—er—competitive in a swimsuit, I suppose,' Meredith continued. 'Women who wear such loose clothing usually have something to hide, don't you think? Poor child. You do understand?'

Oh, I understand, all right, Mandy told herself. I understand that you're a first-class bitch. But you can't expect to take over my husband just because you look like a—like a battleship in heat. I'm starting a new campaign. If I keep my husband thoroughly satisfied every night in our bedroom, he won't have the strength to give *you* a tumble, lady!

'You surprise me,' Meredith continued her grating inquisition. 'I've known Brian for such a long time. He's always been attracted to women who are rather more fully—er—developed.'

You're equating quantity with quality, Mandy giggled to herself. But she had to get out from under this interrogation. She turned to look at the pool. It was the first time she had actually been this close when it was filled. It lay parallel to the ballroom, but was shut off on all sides by staggered wooden walls, which served as wind-screens. The water was a dark blue. She stared into it, mesmerised, both attracted and repelled.

Mandy could remember how, as a little girl, she and her father had played water games. He had been so proud of her when she completed her Junior Red Cross swimming tests. She had loved the water in those long-ago days.

But now there were too many dark shadows in her mind. She struggled with the locked door in her mind, but it would not open. She knew that she feared the water with an unholy passion, but could not remember why. Did not *dare* to remember why.

Warily she backed away from the edge of the pool. Meredith was studying her, seeing the fear gleaming in her eyes, and the frozen look of horror on her face. The older woman got up and disappeared around the edge of the wind-screens. Mandy remained, fighting her fears. And then Himself came out, dressed for dinner.

'Nearly time to eat, dear,' he said. 'Have you been able to relax a little?' She smiled up at him, but was unable to still the quivering of her body. He kissed the tip of her nose.

Why do I doubt that he loves me? she asked herself. But then, I don't. What I doubt—what I fear—is that I'm not enough woman to hold him! Sooner or later the silence may defeat me!

'Will you look at that?' he interrupted. 'The pool's only been filled for two days, and already there's grass in it.' He had his arm around her, and tugged her forward as he moved to the edge of the pool. Her feet were on the concrete lip when her frantic struggling got through to him.

'Hey now,' he said, holding her tightly. 'It's only some junk in the pool!' She struggled harder, beating against his chest with both hands, and making weak mewling noises from deep in her stomach.

'My lord, you're really in a panic. What's the trouble, love?' He swept her up in his arms and carried her away from the pool, back to a metal lawn chair some twenty feet from the water. 'What is it, Mandy?' he pressed her. She clamped a rigid control on her nerves and tried to answer him. Somehow, in the last minutes, she had lost her pad. She tried signs, very slowly, emphasising with facial expressions. 'The water,' she signed, remembering a flash. 'I couldn't get out. I thought I would drown.' She offered him her wrist, where she now wore the Medic-Alert badge as a bracelet. He turned the badge over, and read as if for the first time.

'I should have known,' he muttered, apparently angry with himself. 'Hydrophobia. Fear of water! Oh, my poor, dear Mandy. You're married to a colossal fool!' It hardly seemed proper to agree with him. She ducked her head away to conceal her face. He picked her up out of the chair and sat down himself, resting her in his lap. His hands moved up and down her spine, comforting. Gradually she relaxed and snuggled herself up against him. After a time he got up again, and set her back in the chair. 'Wait here,' he said, 'while I go find us a drink. You'll be OK?' She nodded weakly. He left on his errand of mercy.

After he had gone she began to lecture herself. Amanda Stone, twenty-one years old, and you let yourself go like some silly schoolgirl. No wonder people call you 'child' all the time. She forced her unwilling muscles to lever her up from the chair. Each step towards the water was agony. But she kept it up until she had driven herself to the lip of the pool.

Mandy stopped there, just inches from the edge, letting her eyes roam around the pool itself, but avoiding the water. It took considerably more courage to command herself to look down. The sun was sinking rapidly, and the water was turning dark, more ominous. She stifled her first burst of panic, and, just as she was congratulating her cowardly self, she felt a hand in the middle of her back, pushing her forward inexorably, over the lip of the pool and down into the dark death that reached out to seize her.

Her scream was soundless. Her fears for herself would never be enough for her to force open that tightly closed door in her mind. She hit the water with an awkward splash, barely loud enough to be heard a few feet away, and then her mind broke under the terror. Far in the background, completely divorced from her realities, from her dark, doom-laden world, she heard the baying of a great dog, a bugle of alarm in the evening air.

Mandy paddled desperately in the direction where she thought the air must lie. Water surged into her open mouth, and she gagged on it. Her head broke the surface, silhouetted against the shadows for a moment, then she sank again, soundlessly screaming, locked in her own little cube of silence.

She did not hear the splash as Brian hit the water in a racing dive, fully clothed. Her mind had already given up the struggle and was mercifully blank. She did feel the clutch of his strong hand as she fought him, ruled by panic. He pulled her close, forced them both higher in the water, then his massive fist hit her on the chin.

She was only unconscious for a few minutes, but it was long enough for him to propel her to the shallow end of the pool and lift her out. He stretched her out on the grass, made sure she had not swallowed her tongue, and gave her artificial respiration. The pressure of his hands caused more pain than the water she was spewing up. She waved a weak hand, a cry for mercy. He stopped his ministrations, watched her breathe normally for a time, then gathered her up and started towards the house.

Mrs Duggan met them halfway, her arm full of towels. Brian snatched one, rubbed her face dry, and then her hair. 'What happened, Mandy?' he pleaded. 'I asked you to wait for me. What happened?'

She gestured for him to put her down. She wobbled a step or two, and then regained her composure. Her jaw ached worse than any other part of her. She fingered the pain.

'I had to do something,' he defended himself. 'You were fighting me so hard that you could have drowned us both!'

Aunt Rose came out, attracted by the noise. 'This is a silly time to go swimming, Amanda,' she lectured. 'Dinner is ready to be served. Why are you all laughing at me?'

They moved back to the house, his arms sustaining her. She could feel the water squishing in her shoes. Her blouse was soaked to transparency, clinging to her every curve. The terror had passed, leaving her weak and exhausted, but strangely calm. She looked up at her husband. 'I love you,' she signed.

'I know you do,' he laughed. She stuck out her tongue at him, and he slapped her bottom in reprisal. 'Upstairs and change,' he commanded. 'If you feel like coming down afterwards, do so. If not, I'll bring you up a tray.'

She wobbled up the stairs on his arm, gaining strength as each moment passed. In the bedroom she stood shivering still while he undressed her, stripping off the wet clothes and dumping everything into a wicker basket in the bathroom. Then he pushed her into the hot shower. She balanced herself against the wall, and suddenly he was there with her, his clothes in an untidy pile outside the shower stall. Once again his strong, warm arms held her, warm water sprayed gently over both, and gradually her world came back to normal.

He helped her out of the shower after a time, dried her carefully with two massive towels, then bundled her up and carried her to the bed.

'Stay here for a while,' he commanded. 'Then if you feel you can do it, come down for dinner. OK?'

She signed a 'thank you,' and watched while he quickly dressed in trousers and a black sweater, and went back downstairs. He saved your life, she told herself. What better proof do you need? You didn't need to break silence at any time—they—all the ones who love you—are watching over you! You love him. He loves you. Relax. Go down to dinner. Show him you're a first-class trooper. Up and at 'em, girl.

Her mind was willing, but her legs were weak. Nevertheless, she managed to drive them. They carried her unsteadily over to the wardrobe. The racks which had been so empty for so long were now aflow with a selection of dresses, all kinds, all colours. She had never seen any of them before. Oh, Aunt Rose, she whispered to herself. You wonderful, wonderful woman!

Her hands fumbled down the row of dresses in a delirium of excitement. The choice was too wide. Mandy closed her eyes and made a stab at the rack, coming away with a buttercup-yellow linen shirtwaister, with a ruffle of lace that outlined the deep V-neck. Her bureau disgorged matching yellow briefs, and a half-slip. They fitted to perfection. The hem swung freely just at the knee, but moulded her hips and bodice like a second skin. She made a face at herself in the mirror, and was startled by what she saw. With her curls still wet and clinging, she looked like a sixteen-year-old girl, with twenty-five years of experience. She stopped long enough to use her moisturising cream, and applied a light powdering to conceal the forming bruise on her chin. A touch of mascara, a light gloss for her lips, and she was ready to face the world.

From down at the foot of the stairs her husband was calling for her. Hah! So much for 'We'll wait for you,' she thought, but started obediently down the stairs. He came halfway up to meet her. 'Hey, that's great for around the house,' he admired. 'But don't you dare let me catch you wearing that off the property!' She dropped him a smiling curtsy, and he passed her a small glass. 'Brandy,' he said. 'To restore your spirits. Do they need it?'

She took the glass from him with both hands and sipped at it. Aunt Rose came out of the dining-room to admire her own handiwork. 'Not too bad, Mandy?' she said with a chuckle. 'It certainly seems to destroy the idea that you're a child. Did you try the perfume?'

Mandy shook her head. If there had been perfume, she was too dazed to find it. Mrs Duggan came out from the kitchen. 'My, and what have the little people done with Amanda Stone?' she exclaimed. 'That makes two missing. I can't find Miss Clemson about. Anyone seen her?'

'She may still be out in the garden or the pool,' Brian said. 'You all go in. Mandy and I will take one turn around the garden to let her know we're waiting.'

'Be sure you keep walking, you two,' Mrs Duggan suggested with a broad grin on her face. 'The supper's cold enough as it is.'

Arm in arm they walked out in the garden. Mandy and her husband! Why, how often I think of him that way, she told herself. Or should it be more properly Brian and his wife? She squeezed his arm and giggled to herself. Brian and his biddable wife? He looked down at the concentrated frown on her face, and she knew he was laughing at her. She didn't care.

They both heard the low growl at the same time. 'Liza,' Brian said. The sound came from the other side of the wind-screens. They walked faster, turning the corner together, holding hands. There was a whimper to match the growl. And there in front of them, trapped in the corner where the walls joined, was Meredith Clemson. The front of her dress was torn, and she was quivering with fear. Liza crouched in front of her, growling.

'What's gotten into that dog?' Brian muttered as he moved forward quickly. 'Sit, Liza.' The dog refused the command. Mandy came up beside them. She snapped her fingers to get the dog's attention, then gestured a command. The huge animal gave one more growl, then backed up and sat down.

Meredith made an attempt to run to Brian, but the slight movement of her feet brought Liza up again. The woman backed deeper into the corner.

'Brian?' Her voice was shrill, uncontrolled. Brian stood still. There was a cold look in his eyes, and his forehead was furrowed.

'Why would Amanda's dog hate you so much, Meredith?' he asked, in a very conversational voice.

'How would I know?' the girl screamed at him. 'Just get me out of here.'

'Yes,' he said softly. 'It's a puzzle, isn't it? Did you know that Mandy fell into the pool and almost drowned?'

Meredith's face contorted. 'It's no fault of mine that she can't swim,' she stormed.

'No, I suppose not,' he said, still using that soft voice.

He's thinking about something, Mandy told herself. He's got a bone in his teeth and he'll never let go.

'Mandy,' he said, 'take Liza into the kitchen.' She leaned down for a grip on the dog's collar, and they both walked away. The frightened woman in the corner watched them, looking at the frowning face of the man in front of her, and ran for the house.

CHAPTER NINE

By HARD work Mandy and Jane Brush managed to finish the manuscript at noon three days later. Jane Brush? The day following her unplanned dip in the swimming-pool Mandy had come down to the study late. Her husband had been waiting for her, in none too good a humour.

'Did you forget we have to get this manuscript out in a hurry?' It had been a rhetorical question, on the order of 'And when did you stop beating your wife?'

'No.' Mandy had smiled her sweetest smile as she signed.

'Then you'd better get at it,' he'd grumbled as he pulled out her chair for her.

'No.' Again that sweet smile had accompanied the sign.

'No? Come on, Mandy. Get with it!' His natural 'I am the master of all I survey' tone had been quavering. Mandy had come prepared. She had pulled the little paste-on label out of her pocket and pinned it over her breast.

'On strike—again!' it had said.

'Come on, Amanda!' he'd roared. But for twenty minutes his roaring had made no impression at all on her quiet refusal, until finally he had given up. 'Well, at least tell me what it's all about,' he'd said with a sigh.

'It's about equal rights, and no slavery, and I'd rather be your wife than your secretary. And we could hire a nice girl to help,' she had written in her pad.

'Sure we could,' he'd agreed. 'But it will take a month to find somebody qualified. So you'd better get to it.'

'Jane Brush could help,' she'd signed.

'Jane Brush? The little Brush girl who went to work in Providence for the lawyer?'

'And who came home to look after her mother and needs part-time work,' Mandy had written.

Brian had thrown up his hands. 'Extortion,' he'd muttered. 'All right, go hire the girl. It'll take you a week to find her, I'll bet. Where is she?'

'In the kitchen, waiting,' Mandy had signed. Her husband had looked for a moment as if he were going to cloud up and rain all over her, but then his innate good humour had caught up with him. He had swept Mandy up in a big hug. 'Managing wives,' he'd murmured in her ear, 'I hate them.' But his kiss had not been in any way diminished. And the typing had gone on at full speed.

Unfortunately, in that same length of time, by some means or another, Meredith had been restored to good standing, and the sound of her voice coupled with Brian's at the poolside had driven Mandy's fingers faster than ever.

With great satisfaction she now watched him scan the product, shove it into a mail folder, and seal it up. Mr Rutherford was standing by with the Continental to rush it to the post office in Providence.

'And that's that,' Brian said, very self-satisfied. He gave the appearance of a man who had laboured long and hard over the book, despite the fact that he had spent the last three days out in the sun with *that woman*. Mandy smiled at him. It might have been her fingers that had brought the book up to the wire, but it was his brain that had created it in the first place. It was with a very great deal of satisfaction that she covered her typewriter, filed the tapes and the second copies, and tidied up the room. With a contented sigh, she snapped her fingers. Brian turned to read the message.

Her busy fingers whirled. 'I want you——' she signed.

'Me too!' he interrupted. 'Right now. Let's go upstairs.' She held up both hands in a stop-sign.

'That's not something nice girls do in the afternoon,' she signed.

'Well, a lot you know,' he laughed. 'It's the best time, and the best place—and why am I arguing?' She was swept up in his arms before she knew it, and headed out into the hall. Meredith was coming down the stairs, dressed to kill.

'I'm off to Newport to visit friends, darling,' she purred. 'You'll miss me, I suppose.' That little conniving grin accompanied the words. Meredith at her most effective.

'Have a good trip,' he chuckled. 'Mandy and I have plans of our own.' He started up the stairs. Only Mandy saw the cold chill that sparked in the other woman's eyes as they swept out of sight around the curve of the stairwell. And although the afternoon was all that he had promised, and perhaps more, she could not put that look out of her mind.

The next three weeks passed quickly. Brian was deep in the development of a plot for his new book, tossing out ideas, dialogue, characters, and using Mandy for a sounding-board. He seemed very pleased with the new approach, but Meredith, still hanging in there, was not pleased at all.

'She's restless,' Aunt Rose said one evening at table, when the Clemsons had gone in to Providence for a re-union with old friends. 'If her brother hadn't come for her today I had the feeling she might—well—explode.'

'She's your guest,' Brian responded, 'and she's welcome as long as you want to have her here.'

'But you've never understood why I wanted her here, have you?' his aunt grumbled. 'And at times I wonder myself.'

'I suppose it's just because they're both your god-children,' Brian said. 'You know, of course, that Amanda thinks that Meredith is related to the devil—or someone close to that hierarchy?'

Both aunt and nephew turned to look at her. With that stony Stone look she told herself. But the silent giggles gave her away, and the stony looks became that—supercilious—stare for just under sixty seconds, when they both broke out laughing.

With the dessert, Aunt Rose had another thought. 'Speaking about Meredith,' she sighed, 'I think you both need to—well—be careful. That girl was spoilt rotten by her parents, and when they died she ran wild. She hates to be a loser in anything. And I'm not sure just what she *wouldn't* do if she was crossed. You know, the both of them have just about run through all the family money.'

'We'll be careful,' Brian noted. 'I don't see that she can do us any particular harm. But if she does...' Again that Gallic shrug of the shoulders. 'And now, Aunt Rose, there's a lovely moon, and my wife and I have a date to see our garden by moonlight. You'll excuse us?'

Mandy slept late the next day. The night before they had come up to bed rather early, but sleep had come much later. She lifted her head off the pillow, and then dropped back as the room began to rock and sway. Brian was up already, puttering around in the bedroom. She unglued one sleepy eye and watched him dress. 'I'm a farmer today,' he said. 'The book is finished, and there are just a few odd jobs for my secretary to get at. And there's something else I need to talk to you about, love.'

She nodded, and regretted it immediately. It took two minutes for the world to settle down again. There was definitely something wrong with her machinery. He came over to the bed and sat down beside her, holding her tiny hand in his massive paw. 'It's about your house,' he said, catching her attention at once.

'Something's wrong with my house?'

'No. Not as far as I know. Something's wrong with Mrs Duggan.'

'What is it?' she signed anxiously.

'It's her father, dear. You know she has the care of the old man. He's too old to be left alone, but too young to be a vegetable. He needs to be active.'

'Yes,' she signed, making no attempt to move her head again. 'How can we help?'

'Well, he lives in the suburbs of Providence, in a rented house, with no grounds around it. The old man has outlived all his friends, so there's really nothing for him in the neighbourhood. It's too far from here for Mrs Duggan. She's been commuting every night, but that's asking too much of her. Her father loves to garden and we have a housekeeper we might lose if she has to continue this long-distance commute. We also have a house that I don't really want you to sell, and that house has a garden that very badly needs a gardener. What I would like to do is to move the old man into your house as our caretaker-gardener. We'll pay him a salary, and he can putter around the rose garden and keep it up. He and Mrs Duggan will have a home close by, and we'll have a second house, just in case, in the far future, we should have a child who needs a home. Agreed?'

'Wonderful,' she signed, 'but we have to pay him enough to think he is really wanted.'

'Well, of course. We can't expect him to look after the rose garden without some proper income. I'll take care of that.'

'You are a wonderful man,' she signed.

'Yes, aren't I?' He was grinning like a Cheshire cat, all eyes and mouth and sparkling white teeth. 'And now I have to go help Caleb for a while. Hay, you know.' She blinked her eyes at him, not daring to shake her head in any direction. *Hay?* It didn't seem possible. This urbane spinner of wild tales? This best-selling author? Hay? One more facet of a multi-faceted man, a man whom she must come to understand, and that quickly. Such a wonderful man. As the door closed behind him she dropped off to sleep again with a smile on her face.

It was eleven o'clock before she managed to awaken fully. She felt much better. A simple blue organdy dress would serve for the day. She crept downstairs. Before she quite made it, another attack of nausea seized her and compelled her to sit down. Her head rested against the coolness of the heavy mahogany banister, and voices from all over the house filtered into her ear. In the kitchen, Aunt Rose and Becky were discussing dresses, their language punctuated by giggling. In the study Brian was carrying on a conversation with Meredith. Mandy desperately wanted to snoop, and no amount of 'nice girls don't do that' was going to stop her.

'I don't understand you, Brian,' Meredith said, using her most caressing tone. 'You wanted me in Europe. You chased me all over the continent, as I remember.'

'Yes,' Brian admitted. 'And caught you more than once. But that was two years ago. I wanted you pretty badly in those days.'

'Well, now I'm available.'

'You were always available,' he snorted. 'And now I'm not.'

'Why should that be?' Her voice became more shrill. 'Surely you can't take seriously a marriage to that—that child?'

'There's a difference between wanting and loving,' he replied.

'Is there really? Give me your hand. There. Has she anything like that? Don't tell me it doesn't do something to you.'

'Let's not kid each other, Meredith. Sure, I felt something. Disgust. Listen, Amanda is young, and she doesn't have all your plush curves, but when I touch her I know I'm the only man who has ever done that. With you it's like standing in line at some check-out counter. With Mandy I get love, admiration, respect, companionship, obedience, and some day a son—I hope. And let me tell you something else, Meredith. She loves me, and I love her. And she's a demure little miss in the kitchen, but under the bed sheets she's a wildcat. Does that satisfy your curiosity?'

Meredith stormed out of the study, her teeth clenched and her eyes sparking fire. Mandy squeezed hard against the banister, trying to keep out of sight. Brian came out a moment later, and she stood up to greet him. He swept her off the stairs, kissed her, and set her down on the floor. Her stomach rebelled for a second, and then was back in order.

'I'm going into the city,' he said. 'I've an appointment with those lawyers of yours. Now that we've settled about the house, I think it's time for me to settle up those little odds and ends of the rest of your—dowry. You feel OK?'

'I did until just this minute,' she signed.

'That's too bad, dear,' he replied absent-mindedly. She could see that he wasn't paying attention, that his mind was on other things.

'There are sharks in the swimming-pool,' she signed.

'Of course,' he replied as he ruffled her hair. 'Don't go until I get back. Try to get some lunch down you— you've missed breakfast. I won't be long.' She nodded, put her hands behind her, closed her eyes, and offered her lips. 'Greedy,' he murmured, but he kissed her all the same and walked away whistling.

Mandy shuffled out into the kitchen, where Rose and Mrs Duggan fluttered at her. Tea and sympathy, Mandy thought. The cure for anything. She shivered, and Aunt Rose noticed. 'What's the matter now?' she asked. 'More man trouble again?'

Mandy shook her head and picked up the kitchen slate. 'Brian has gone to see my lawyer about my dowry,' she wrote.

'Dowry?' Aunt Rose giggled. 'That has such an old-fashioned sound about it. Delicious. Is there something wrong with it?'

'Yes. He's a very proud man.'

'Of course he is,' Mrs Duggan contributed. 'All real men are, dearie.' She eyed Mandy speculatively. 'Is there something wrong?'

'I don't want to talk about it,' Amanda scribbled. 'I was sick this morning.' An absolute silence settled over the kitchen.

'Do you say so?' Mrs Duggan said. Her slight brogue was tremendously amplified.

'Oh, my—Amanda!' Aunt Rose said. Becky left the sink to come over and listen.

'It doesn't mean anything,' Amanda scribbled glumly. 'It's only one day.'

'OK,' Mrs Duggan laughed. 'Let's talk about babies.'

'Blonde, with blue eyes,' Aunt Rose said dreamily. 'A lovely little girl. Wouldn't that be nice?'

'Don't be saying that,' Mrs Duggan objected. 'The little people are always listening. It *has* to be a boy. A fine little boy to look like Himself, and carry on the name.'

'Twins?' Rose suggested. 'Saves a lot of argument, don't you think, Amanda?' But the Party of the First Part had nothing to say. She folded her legs up into the chair, hugged herself happily, and giggled soundlessly.

Lunch was a home-made clam chowder. She managed to hold it down with little trouble, hoping against hope that this morning sickness would pass quickly. If it stretches on and on, until I get too big and clumsy, however will I satisfy Brian? she asked herself.

Aunt Rose went up for her afternoon nap right after lunch. Mrs Duggan planned a shopping trip into the city. Mandy washed the lunch dishes, but kept close to the door that led out to the garden. Liza came stomping in for her noon feed, then lay down in the centre of the floor, so the girl had to continually step over her or walk around. And all this time there was an air of expectancy hanging over the kitchen. Mandy sat down over another cup of coffee, ear cocked to the front door, and day-dreamed about what she had overheard.

A wildcat in bed, he had said. Am I really? she wondered. It certainly doesn't sound the sort of thing a nice girl would do. But it was extremely hard to be a 'nice girl' when he ran his fingers up across her breasts and down her thighs. And just because she wiggled against him, and wrapped her legs around him, and bit him on occasion, that really wasn't being *too* wanton, was it? She had not worked out the answer when she heard him come in.

The front door slammed with a mighty crash. Mandy jumped a dozen feet in the air, and put one hand on the knob of the kitchen door. 'Amanda! Amanda damn Stone!' he roared. 'Where the hell are you, woman? Three hundred thousand dollars of dowry? I'll wring your neck! Amanda!'

It's worse than I expected, Amanda told herself glumly. She grabbed at Liza's collar and scooted for the door. Then she stopped to reconsider. There was no use making things worse than they were. A complete disappearance would only add fuel to the fire. She went back to the table, scrubbed the slate clean, and wrote, 'Taking Liza for a long walk.' On second thoughts, she underlined the word *long*.

She could hear him stomping down the hall, trying every door in passing, and slamming each one behind him. She took Liza's collar again, slipped quietly out of the back door, and dashed for the fringe of the apple orchard. Liza padded along under protest, not pleased at the rush which disturbed her digestion. When they gained the shelter of the trees Amanda stopped to catch her breath and looked back at the house.

Well, she told herself, you've done it again! But when there's a bad thunderstorm coming, only a fool stands around waiting for the lightning to hit! With this bit of home-spun philosophy firmly in mind, she followed Liza up through the orchard, and then circled back down to the beach again.

They walked almost an hour along the beach, until they came to the mouth of the river, and were facing the ocean. Lovely sparkling shells crammed the narrow beach area, and were added to her collection. Once she tried throwing sticks for Liza to chase, but the old dog sat down at her side and refused to participate in such puppy foolishness. When they came to Demorest Point they found two little boys digging for clams. Mandy checked her watch, then squatted down in the sand to observe. The boys were small, and the clams smaller, but it made a pleasant interlude, and perhaps Brian would have cooled off before she got back?

In the middle of all this daydreaming it suddenly came to her that she was walking on the beach in one of her new dresses, instead of her jeans. And besides, it was late enough now for her to go back and face the music. It can't be all that bad, she mused, smiling. He can't kill me over a little money problem. Still smiling, she pulled her special ultrasonic dog whistle out of her pocket and blew it. Nothing happened.

Liza is either too far away to hear, or too busy to obey, she thought. The poor lady didn't want to come along in the first place. Maybe she knew something I don't know—maybe she's gone home to make a separate peace with Brian? That thought brought on a little silent chuckle. She waved a goodbye to the boys, and started back up the hill, headed for home. A lone seagull, temporarily parked on a large rock outcrop, stared at her as she went by. The afternoon was turning muggy. Two or three clouds hastened by on their way to rain on New Bedford, just over the horizon. She watched them reflectively, thinking it perhaps might have been better for her to go that far too.

With a little more purpose she started up the hill, heading for the clear ridge, the steep cliffs, whose barren area made well for walking. A few more clouds came up, halting over the Point, obscuring the sun. The day became even darker. Mandy had reached the summit of the ridge before she heard the voice calling her. Meredith Clemson, a small figure in the distance, yelling at the top of her voice, pointing over the cliff, dancing up and down. Mandy broke into a fleet-footed run, covering the distance as quickly as she could. From far down in the fields she could hear the noise of Caleb's tractor at work. Nothing else.

'Amanda,' the other woman yelled as she got within hearing range. 'Over the top of the cliff!'

Mandy panted to a stop, not quite understanding, and unable to question. Meredith had avoided all the sign-lessons, and Mandy had forgotten her writing pad. 'Your dog,' Meredith finally managed. 'Liza. I was standing back there——' she waved down the hill a few yards, to where a clump of trees offered shelter '—and she came running up the hill like a Cossack, chasing a little rabbit ahead of her. They both went over the cliff right there.'

Anxious, Mandy turned to look. 'Right there' was a declivity, almost a tunnel, that led to one of the most precipitous sections of the cliff. She moved forward, stretched out on her stomach, and peered over the edge. A rudimentary trail led down for a few feet—perhaps ten or fifteen—at an extremely steep angle, and ended on a tiny ledge in front of the mouth of a cave. Liza was not in sight.

'There's a cave down there,' Meredith shrilled excitedly. 'She must be in the cave. And there's no way that she could get back up that steep slope. It's too slippery!'

Mandy assessed the situation as calmly as she could. Liza, trapped on a ledge above that mad sea, and a change of weather coming up. There had to be help. Someone would have to go down after her—and *someone* else would have to go for help. A heavy rope would do it! She stood up and signed at Meredith, to no avail. Simple signs would have to do.

Mandy pointed to herself. 'Me,' she mouthed, and pointed down the path to the ledge. 'You.' She pointed at Meredith, and then down the side of the hill to where the tractor noises were still to be heard. 'Go,' she mouthed. 'Bring help.'

The other woman nodded eagerly. 'You'll go down after the dog,' she confirmed, 'and then I'll go back to the farm?' Mandy nodded and turned back to the cliff. There was really only one way to do it. She would have to slide down the path, and trust to luck that her feet landed on the ledge. And I'd rather not watch, she told herself as she lay down on her stomach and gradually wiggled her way backwards into the narrow notch.

Meredith had been right about one thing. The path was slippery. In fact, she had to slow her descent by snatching at the patches of saw grass that lined the sides. In slow, tortured jerks she went down, until at last, twelve feet below the top of the cliff, her feet landed with a solid thump on the projecting rock that made up the ledge. With her eyes closed she practised a little deep breathing until she had regained total control of her body.

At that point she waved to Meredith, whose head could just barely be seen peering over the edge. The other woman was laughing, a cruel sound that echoed off the cliff and scattered a nest of starlings. Hurry up, Mandy screamed silently.

The other woman waved a hand. 'I told you you couldn't hold Brian,' she yelled down. 'Have a good night!' And with that Meredith got up, dry-washed her hands, and slowly sauntered off.

Oh, my living lord, Mandy told herself, what have I gotten myself into now? She turned around towards the shelter of the cave. There was none. She was anchored on a ledge no more than four feet wide, and perhaps fifteen feet long, and not a bit of shelter was included. Down below, in almost all directions, the ocean waves were being blanketed by the approaching fog.

Wearily she sagged back against the rock wall of the cliff. Out at sea, under lowering skies, a line of three fishing-boats were rounding the point, heading for shelter. They were too far out to see her, and probably weren't looking in any case. Twelve feet above her head was safety, and no way to get there. Or was there?

She edged her way back to the trail, and tried to force her way up. A few inches, no more, and her feet slipped, dropping her back to the ledge. She tried again, digging her fingers into the scrabbled earth. Every inch upward brought a shower of gravel and dirt down. The saw grass was beyond reach, hugging the last foot or two below the top of the cliff. She dangled for a moment, barely a foot above the ledge, and then her fingers weakened.

She collapsed back on to the ledge, one leg hanging over it—over the drop to the sea. Mandy edged her way back on to solid rock, and sat against the wall. The tips of her fingers were bleeding. Her legs were scratched, and her dress was beyond repair. There was no escape by herself. She huddled into the smallest bundle she could make, to hide from the chill of the fog.

Why would Meredith have done such a thing? she agonised. Sooner or later someone is bound to find me, and then what? Are they bound to find you? her inner voice asked cruelly. If they stand up there at the very track you came down, are they bound to find you? Can you yell up to them, get their attention? Just the mention of yelling jolted her. The dark little door in her mind opened a crack. She could smell the African smoke. She shuddered. Not even to save her life could she yell. The door closed with a thud.

The bottom dropped out of her confidence. All the years of training—'you're just like all the other people, Amanda, only you speak a different language' —well, it was all proving to be a lie, wasn't it? You're not like all the other people, Amanda, and you never will be! Never! So you might as well stop kidding yourself. But you do have one advantage, girl. If they don't find you, you don't have to face the long end on this damn ledge— you can always just step over the side, and it will be all over in a couple of minutes.

She huddled deeper into herself as the night set in. The fog settled, a heavy sea-fog, shutting off all visibility. Thirst was assailing her—thirst and hunger, even though she had eaten lunch not nine or ten hours before. Thirst—that would be the great limiter. If only Brian would come. Brian, she screamed soundlessly.

Gradually she withdrew into herself, abandoned all connection with the outside. Ignored the chill, forgot the fog, and dreamed that Brian was coming. It might have been about eight o'clock, with the fog heavy on the land, when she heard the searchers. Dogs barked, men yelled. And Caleb, almost over her head, cautioned, 'Back off, Brian. You can't even see the edge. It's a long way down from here!'

'She's got to be here,' Brian yelled. 'Liza's come directly to this point. You take the men south.' Silence, a long silence, broken only by the occasional fall of pebbles on her head. Mandy prayed, and moved under the shelter of the little cave. 'Mandy? Mandy, for heaven's sake make a noise, Mandy!'

She tried to scream. Tried and failed. She feared that opening door in her mind more than she feared death. Tears began to run fecklessly down both cheeks. And then she heard a spurt of pebbles as Brian's foot struck a loose pile of dirt, a muttered curse, a rush of dirt and debris, and a distinct thud.

For an endless moment Amanda hugged the cliff. Then, with more guts than common sense, she ventured out on to the ledge. A body lay there, too quietly, her mind screamed. Her hands raced up to its head. Brian, they reported immediately. Brian. Not moving.

And now you have to do something, Amanda Stone, she told herself. Her teeth chattered, but not from cold. Now you have to do something. He may be dead. If not yet, he may die. You can lie here in the night, he can't! You have to scream. While the men are still close by, you have to scream! Just thinking the thought was enough to open the door on her memory. She was overwhelmed with fear and guilt and remembrance. But you have to keep your head, she shouted at herself. For Brian, you have to keep your head.

And despite the fear that racked her, despite the smell and the sound and the fury of death shaking at her being, Amanda Stone did something she had not contemplated for all those years. She took a deep breath, leaned back, and screamed. Pitifully at first, a bare whimper, then growing louder, until it swelled and groped for the heavens.

People heard and yelled, and moved in her direction, and the fog began to lift, both in her mind and in her world. Until she collapsed, smiling.

CHAPTER TEN

MANDY was so terribly sleepy, and the two men talking by her bed were disturbing her. She turned on her side, wishing there were some way she could yell at them to go away. Her movement silenced them. She dropped back into the cocoon of dreams, and a tiny smile played at her lips.

'You'll do,' Dr Hinson told Brian. 'Just a quick knock-out. Go gently for a day or two. And she'll do too. A tough little bird is our Amanda. Just a little bit of damage.'

What damage? Amanda's eyes snapped open. Brian was looking down at her, like some pirate. There was a plaster behind his right ear, and a conspicuous bump on his forehead.

'Lord, Mandy,' he said. His voice was husky, full of care and tiredness. 'Mandy——' It seemed to be all he could say with his voice, but his body, his hands, his eyes—they all gave her the message she wanted to know. He held her close, cherishing her as only a lover could. It was enough for the moment. She clung to him desperately, and then satisfied, relaxed.

'A few scratches and bruises,' Dr Hinson rambled on. 'And one tremendous sore throat. No more talking for a few days, Mandy. Oh, and the baby's all right.' Brian seemed to have missed the *baby* bit.

'What happened?' she signed, trying to divert his attention.

'Well, I got over being mad about two o'clock. Three hundred thousand dollars, Amanda?' She blushed and ducked her head. 'But we're living on *my* money,' he continued. She nodded, thoroughly subdued. 'By six o'clock I really began to worry about you. Nobody had seen you leave the house. All I could think of was what a damn fool I was yelling for you like that—well, that's another story. I thought you had gone into hiding somewhere, but with Liza with you, what could go wrong? So I waited. Along about three o'clock, Liza came dragging up to the house, sick as a dog. No pun intended. That really shook me up.'

'Liza sick? I couldn't find her!' she signed.

'Well that made two of us. Liza was sick, and you were missing. I called Doc Petty, the veterinarian, and rushed Liza over to his shop. Caleb began to muster up the neighbours to look for you. I never knew a girl who could be so much trouble to find, Amanda Stone!' He said it, but the words were warm, and love looked through his eyes. And now, she realised, she felt sure of him, and of herself.

'I'm worth the looking for,' she signed.

'Damned if you're not!' He got up and kissed her again, gently, firmly, lovingly. Feeling ten thousand times better, Mandy clung to him for just that extra second before his muscles rebelled, and he sank back into a chair.

'Liza?' she prompted.

'Yes, well, they found out pretty quickly she'd been doped. Somebody fed her a raw hamburger, with a pill inside. Doc Petty pumped her out and purged her, and I took her home. While everybody was out searching, Liza just curled up on her rug by the kitchen door, and snored. But we couldn't find a trace of you. Not a trace.'

'Where was Meredith?' signed Mandy.

'Meredith? Why—I don't remember. She was around the house all the time. I remember she helped put Aunt Rose to bed. Rose was in a total state of panic, let me tell you.'

'So then what happened,' she wanted to know.

'Then Liza woke up, took a few groggy steps around the kitchen sniffing at us all, and then went dashing up the stairs. She checked every bedroom, and then came down, whining, scratching at the back door. So I let her out, and we followed her. Straight back to the beach, she went, and then up the ridge. It was a tough scent to trace. We're lucky the rain held off—it would have washed everything away. And when she took us to the edge of the cliff I thought I'd drop dead, right on the spot. Oh, Mandy, you've no idea how dark life seemed at that moment. I thought sure you'd gone over the cliff. But the fog was too dense, and Liza wasn't exactly sure of the scent, so I sent her off with the others—and then like a fool slipped at the cliff-edge——'

'And fell into my lap,' she teased with her signs.

'And fell right into your lap,' he chuckled. 'I hear tell that Caleb heard you screaming. He brought up the tractor and the lights, and they fished us out. End of tale.'

'Oh, my dear,' she signed, tears in her eyes. 'Oh, my dear!' He came to her again, burying his face in her hair. After all those years in the rose garden, clutching life privately and desperately to herself, she found it hard to confide her innermost thoughts to someone else. Please, God, she prayed, let him love me enough for this.

'I love children,' she said with her hands.

'As I do, love. Wait a darn minute. The doctor said something——'

'The baby,' she interrupted. 'I—you're not angry?'

'I thought I said something about pills,' he said. 'Didn't you get the pills?'

'Yes, I got the pills,' she signed carefully. 'But you never said I had to *take* them, so I didn't.'

It was hard to believe, but he was laughing at her. She fumbled for words. 'I've really only known one man—you. All those other women, they all had so much to give you. They could talk, and sing, and tell you how they love you. When you married me I was so afraid that you did it to spite Meredith.' He was shaking his head as she signed, disagreeing with all her conclusions. She ploughed doggedly on. 'I wanted to tie you to me,' she continued. 'I wanted to put a chain on you—a baby. That's how I felt at first. I was selfish. Are you angry?'

'Angry?' He laughed. 'Mandy, I'm so pleased with you—not just because of the baby, but because I'm finally seeing the real you. But you said that's how you felt at first?'

'After you—you saved my life at the swimming-pool,' she signed, 'I felt that maybe you just might love me. And then I wanted a baby more than before. I wanted to make you a gift that none of those other women could give you. Have they?' She looked at him anxiously.

'Have they what?'

'Given you a child?' she signed.

'No, sweetheart.' She frowned at him. He ruffled her hair and kissed her forehead.

'Besides,' she signed. 'I love children. Your children.'

'So now it's plural,' he chuckled. 'Is this a long-term campaign?'

'I thought four would be nice,' she signed, 'but Aunt Rose said that two were more than enough.'

'Aunt Rose,' he said gloomily. 'We're having babies to order according to Aunt Rose's requirements? You talked the whole thing over with her, and never even gave me a whisper?'

She put her hand to her mouth, a startled expression on her face. That was exactly what she had done, blissfully unaware that she was making the bear angry. Dummy! she yelled at herself.

'I was going to tell you,' she signed.

'When?'

'Just as soon as I found a day when I had plenty of courage and you weren't grouching, and I hadn't done anything else particularly stupid,' she signed dejectedly.

He swept her up out of her chair and held her close and warm. She opened one eye and looked up at his face. He was smiling! She tucked her head in under his chin and wiggled herself closer. It wasn't as hard to tell him as you thought, she lectured herself. Besides being your lover, he's so—so nice!

'Now tell me the important thing,' he said gently. 'Amanda Stone can talk—well, not very well, but—— Tell me.'

And so she did. All about Africa, the raid, her mother's warning, the lake. Told it all as memories came painlessly through the little open door in her mind, and flowed down to her talking fingers.

'I told you,' Dr Hinson said. 'Psychosomatic!'

'Will it return?' he asked anxiously.

'Not unless you duplicate the original circumstances. I'd keep her out of Africa, if I were you.'

'Yes, I can take a hint,' Brian agreed as he hugged Mandy, cradling her gently against his shoulder for several long minutes.

Eventually he kissed the top of her nose and put her down. 'Now then, Mrs Stone, there are people downstairs. I had invited a few people for dinner tonight. My agent and his wife——'

'And Meredith?' she interrupted. He gave her a curious look.

'And Meredith,' he agreed. 'But you can stay up here. I'll bring you——'

'No, I can't,' she interrupted again. 'I'm the hostess in this house. And I have special reasons for being there. Scoot out and let me get a little more rest.'

Dinner was scheduled for seven-thirty that night, with cocktails beforehand. Mandy stayed in her room, consulting with her household staff, purposely missing the drinks. When all her instructions were understood, she slipped into her new linen suit, a front-pleated pink skirt, a cotton-blended floral print blouse with a stand-up ruffled collar, with a self-fabric bow, and simple white blazer with double pockets. Demure, that was what she wanted.

Her auburn curls glistened after brushing. She added a light eye-liner, a touch of moisturiser, a pink lip-gloss, and was ready for battle. The others had already come to the table when she slipped into the room and took up her chair at its foot.

Brian looked resplendent, at the head of the table. Mrs Frank was at his left, with her husband next to her. Meredith Clemson was on his right, with Aunt Rose between her and Mandy. The meal went slowly, a warm soup for the cool night, steaks done to order, mixed vegetables from the farm. Two flower arrangements, all blossoms from the garden which Mandy had rebuilt, had pride of place as a centrepiece.

The conversation was slow and desultory. Meredith, normally the life of any dinner party, was particularly subdued. She kept glancing out of the corner of her eye at Mandy, while trying to keep Brian in play. Dessert was a huge strawberry shortcake, a prize New England tradition, overloaded with whipped cream and oozing strawberry juices. Mrs Duggan bore it in, setting it all in front of Brian. As she went out she stopped and whispered something in Mandy's ear. Mandy nodded, and the housekeeper left the room, a big smile on her face. Meredith had her hand on Brian's arm, making some point in their private conversation. Mandy sat stiffly in her chair and counted up to one hundred, letting her anger build. It was time to begin.

She pushed back her chair and stalked around the table to Brian's side. The conversation died away. She snapped her fingers at him, and then signed a message. He looked startled. She repeated the gesture.

'My wife——' He looked up at the seething anger in her eyes. 'Amanda has something that she wants you all to hear. She asks that I translate it for her.'

Around the table there was a rustle of noise as cutlery was laid down. 'Oh, how charming,' Meredith gushed. She still had her hand on Brian's arm. 'And now the dumb speak? How interesting. I wish I had the brains to understand all that stupid hand-wiggling.'

Mandy signed to Brian. 'My wife says——' He stopped. 'I can't say that sort of thing, Amanda,' he protested. She snapped her fingers under his nose, a grim expression on her face. 'Well, maybe I can,' he decided. 'My wife says, Meredith, that if you don't get your hands off her husband, she will scratch your eyes out.'

Meredith screeched. 'That stupid bitch can't talk to me like that.'

Mandy signed again.

'My wife says, Meredith, that if you would wash all that dye and bleach out of your hair you would stop poisoning your brain, and you might understand simple things much more easily.'

'Brian,' Meredith shrilled at him, 'you certainly can't let her talk to me like that. I'm leaving tomorrow if you don't put a stop to this. I told you she was a mean little bitch!'

'Amanda is entitled to have her say,' Brian said quietly. 'Just because she can't say it the way you and I do, it doesn't mean she isn't to be heard.' Mandy signed again. Brian looked surprised, but translated. 'My wife says that she didn't really mind when your brother attacked her.' He stopped and searched Amanda's face. She continued her message. 'My wife says she doesn't mind your wrecking the study with your temper tantrums,' he translated. Again he stopped and looked up at Mandy. Meredith seemed to be frozen in her chair. Mandy continued. 'My wife says she didn't mind your trying to steal her husband, because she knew it couldn't be done.' Brian smiled up at her after that one. 'My wife says she didn't mind when you pushed her into the swimming-pool, or when you tricked her into going down on to that ledge on the cliff——' Brian stopped in mid-translation. 'You're sure?' he asked Mandy. She nodded impatiently, and gestured for him to continue as her flashing fingers went on.

'My wife says,' he translated very slowly, 'but when you tried to poison her dog, that made her extremely angry!'

Meredith pushed back her chair from the table. 'You can't prove it was me,' she snarled. Mandy reached into the pocket of her blazer and pulled out a plastic container, the size of a prescription bottle. She showed it to Brian, then threw it down on the table in front of Meredith. It banged into her dessert plate.

'My wife says,' Brian said slowly, 'that a witness saw you. She also says that you don't have to worry about leaving tomorrow, because you're going right now. She says that your bag has been packed, the car's at the door, and you're on your way!'

Meredith moved back from the table. 'I'd like to see that crazy little dummy make me!' she screamed. All her sophisticated veneer had disappeared, leaving her face raw and wrinkled with anger.

Brian looked up at Mandy. 'Don't you think this is a little uncivilised, Amanda?' She nodded in agreement, her anger spreading to include him as well as Meredith. 'And don't you think we can talk this over sensibly?'

She glared at him. He started to get up, then thought better of it. 'But——' he started to say. Amanda Stone leaned over the table and picked up the soggy platter that still contained more than half of the strawberry shortcake and its juices. Very gently, she pushed the entire plateful into her husband's face. Then she stalked around the table to Meredith's seat, and pointed towards the door.

Meredith began to curse in a high-pitched, uncontrolled voice. As she backed away she threw her water glass at Mandy, then stepped closer and swung her right hand in a high, arching sweep, trying to slap Mandy's face. But that one, giving thanks again to her martial-arts training, ducked under the swinging arm, grabbed the wrist, and twisted the arm around and back up behind Meredith's shoulders.

Having established her wrestler's wristlock, Mandy pushed the other woman towards the dining-room door. Meredith struggled, but found it impossible to break the hold. Mrs Duggan was standing at the front door. She opened it and bowed as Mandy forced the struggling Meredith through and out on to the tiny porch. Mr Rutherford was outside, standing by the open door of the Continental. Mitchell stood at his side, growling.

Mandy hustled her victim forward and propelled her with a final push into the back seat. Meredith tried to come back out, still screeching, but the dog moved to the open door and growled. The woman withdrew into the furthest corner of the seat and huddled there. Mr Rutherford closed the door, tipped his hat to the indisputable mistress of all she surveyed, and climbed into the driver's seat. He waved one hand as he spun the back wheels, and the car lurched down the driveway. Mandy watched until it reached the curve and disappeared from sight. Meredith's curses were still ringing in her ears.

She stopped at the front door to control the shaking of her hands. Reaction was setting in. Reaction, and shock. There was still one more dragon to face. She took ten deep breaths to steady herself, and headed for the dining-room. Mrs Duggan, still at the front door, applauded as Mandy went by, then closed the door and followed the little figure back down the hall.

Mandy stopped again at the dining-room door. Her anger had vanished, leaving a painful emptiness in her stomach. Her arms trembled. She nibbled at her lip for a second, and went in. Mrs Duggan came in quietly behind her, and dropped into the vacant seat at the foot of the table. Mr and Mrs Frank were sitting quietly, mouths half open. Aunt Rose was trying to find something interesting to watch in the distance. Brian was dabbing at the mess of shortcake which dribbled over his neck, his shirt, and his trousers.

You're for it now, Amanda Stone, she told herself. That strawberry shortcake was definitely not in the script, and improvising has gotten you in over your head again. You have really blown it this time, girl!

Brian pushed his chair back and stood up. 'My wife and I have some—things to discuss,' he rumbled in an enigmatic voice. 'Perhaps you would all share coffee, and excuse us?' He came around the table, took Mandy's arm, and hurried her out of the room and up the stairs. At the landing he stopped.

'You enjoyed throwing Meredith out?' he asked gently.

'Yes.' She managed to croak the word as she stood solemnly in front of him, hands behind her back.

'And you enjoyed even more doing me in with the cake?'

'Oh, yes.' Her voice was unable to carry the tension. Her hands whipped around almost under his nose. 'Oh, ever so immensely!'

He grinned down at her, took her arm again, and hurried her along up the stairs. 'I think we'll have to

have a few words about *sweet* and *biddable*,' he mused
as he guided her into their bedroom.

Behind them in the dining-room, Aunt Rose broke the
silence. 'Ethel,' she called, 'to hell with the coffee. Bring
us a bottle of his best brandy, and we'll all drink a toast.'
Mrs Duggan laughed, and went out in pursuit of a bottle.
It was a quick round trip.

'Pull up a chair, Ethel,' Aunt Rose invited. 'Put your
feet up. Here's to all of us, and to a nice night's work.
Cheers.' They all sipped. 'Pour another round, Ethel,'
Aunt Rose continued, standing up by her chair. 'I
propose another toast—to the taming of the Playboy of
the East. I think I can safely pack up and go back to
Florida in the morning.'

'Do you say so?' Mrs Duggan returned, throwing the
brandy to the back of her throat and smacking her lips.

'What a hell of a book *this* would make,' Mr Frank
said, following suit. 'Come on, Poochy, drink up. I'm
sorry we have to go home before the next act.'

CHAPTER ELEVEN

ROSE SHARON STONE was born at 3:17 a.m., Eastern Standard Time, in the city of Fall River, Massachusetts, on the twenty-second of April. It was a difficult day. In fact, it had been a difficult month.

All through March Mandy had found herself becoming more and more placid. Like a cow chewing her cud, she told Brian. Nothing fitted her, and she hated to sleep on her back, but that part of life had become acceptable. Speaking was something in which she was not yet fully qualified. A few words, a sentence or two, all that was possible. But her lips and tongue felt grotesquely large, and, although she practised under Brian's watchful eye, she still preferred to sign her larger emotions. It was like having a foreign language, a secret code, that only she and Brian knew.

The season edged into April. Brian gave up work on his new book to be with her, and enrolled in the natural childbirth classes. One thing bothered her.

'We live so far from the hospital,' she signed when he pressed her. 'What if we can't get there in time?'

The next day, when she went out for her prescribed walk, Caleb was out on the front porch with a stop-watch in hand, peering down the drive. 'Himself,' he commented when she questioned. 'Wants to know the quickest route to the hospital. Been practising for six days, he has.' When Brian wheeled up the drive ten minutes later she was secretly pleased.

'Forty minutes at the outside,' he told her. 'Well, thirty actually, but we have to make allowances for bad weather, traffic, and things like that. Does it make you feel better?'

It did, of course, and she thanked him properly with her croaky deep voice. Thackery Point was a tiny village, with neither hospital nor clinic, located equidistant between New Bedford, and Fall River. They had elected to go to the old mill city, Fall River. His concern did relieve her mind, and it wasn't until the initial back pains started that she finally broke down and told him the *real* problem.

'Suppose the baby can't talk?' she signed.

'*She* wouldn't dare,' he laughed. 'There's nothing wrong with your vocal cords, love. That's all behind you. In another six months you'll be talking up a storm. And so will our daughter.' It all seemed logical at the time, and set her worries to rest.

The pains actually awakened her shortly before midnight. She lay quietly, her eyes on her wristwatch, until they got closer. At twelve-thirty she nudged Brian. He vaulted out of bed, running, before he had his eyes open.

'Time to go?' he asked, puttering around as if she were a porcelain doll. She smiled at him, pointed to her bag, and started to limp out of the door. He tapped her on the shoulder. 'It might be better if you would put on *both* your shoes. Then you might be able to walk on an even keel!'

The car was waiting at the front door. The sky was spitting rain, and promised a blustery April storm. He cursed every foot of the way, fighting for speed up slippery Route 88, and doing his best to bounce between the pot-holes on Presidential Avenue. Each bounce brought her closer to catastrophe, and it showed on her perspiration-covered face. He noticed, and patted her comfortingly on the knee.

That's about the only pattable part of me available, Mandy laughed weakly to herself. I'm a great big inflated balloon! The pains were sharp, and too close together now for comfort. For a moment she felt fright. 'Breathing,' he reminded her. It was enough to recall the classroom instructions. When they went by the intersection of Route 6 she tried to tell him to go faster, but he needed no telling. She settled back in the seat and tried to hang on.

They drove up under the shelter of the portico of the main hospital building. He left the engine running. 'I'll take you in and park the car later,' he said. His face looked impassive and unconcerned, but the hand he tucked under her arm was shaking. 'It'll be all right, Amanda,' he assured her.

'I know it will,' she signed as they moved through the lighted lobby. 'But somebody is liable to steal the car.'

'To hell with the car,' he blurted out, his cool disappearing. They moved slowly across the lobby to the lifts. She had gained twenty-one pounds during her pregnancy, and felt like a blimp being walked across the landing-field to the hangar.

Up on the third floor he handed her over to the nursing team, and went out in the hall to wait. She watched his back disappear, wishing mightily that it need not be so. It was not just that he was her communication with the world; it was more because he had become a close and necessary part of her being.

The preparation room was crowded. 'Busy night tonight,' laughed the nurse who helped her undress, and supervised the prep work. 'Up behind those storm-clouds is a full moon!'

The nurse bustled off, leaving Mandy resting on a wheeled litter. The pains were close, too close. She tried to signal someone, but the room was too full, too busy. She had nothing to write with, nothing to throw, so she lay back and clenched her fists until the nails bit into her palms. Without particular thought she found herself reciting the twenty-third psalm.

One of the hurrying aides came close. Mandy managed to tug at the woman's uniform trousers. The aide turned and looked. Bells went off. People ran. Somebody snatched at the end of her litter and pushed her out into the hall, on the way to the delivery-room. Instantly Brian's strong hand was in hers, his courage and strength flowing up her arm and into her heart. She essayed a weak smile.

'Great day in the morning!' she heard him yell. 'Where the hell is the doctor?' It was not his most gentle voice. Listeners on the steps of the State House, sixty miles away, could have heard him with no trouble at all. But at least he's here, she thought happily.

A harried doctor burst on the scene. An impatient voice kept saying, 'Hold on, Mrs Stone!' But Mrs Stone had had enough of 'holding on,' and was not in a mood to co-operate. Instead, she took a deep breath, and pushed. Which was why Rose Sharon Stone was born in the corridor, ten feet short of the delivery-room.

He was waiting in her room when they wheeled her back, tired, shaken, elated, and thoroughly scrubbed up. 'Did you see the baby?' she signed eagerly.

'Did I see her?' he crowed, 'I practically delivered her! Oh, lord, Mandy, she's so—so small. Are you all right?'

'Of course I am,' Mandy croaked. 'Tired, but all right. She's small but perfect. Seven pounds, two ounces. Us Smalls know how to do it, don't we? Marvellous. They'll bring her down in a few minutes. You have to put on the mask.'

'What do you know?' he asked nobody in particular as he struggled to don the face mask. 'The second perfect female in our family!'

'Of course,' she signed. 'Look who her father is.' It was just the statement needed to puff up his shattered nerves. I think he might have had more trouble with this birth than I did, Mandy chuckled to herself. But that's what it's all about. How to manage the male animal. Mamma was right. If I wasn't so sore, I'd laugh!

She was in hospital for four days. He came early and stayed late. Mandy recovered her strength quickly. She loved those intimate moments when he sat by the bed while she nursed the child. They did have a little disagreement about names.

'Not her first name,' he maintained stoutly. 'That's Rose—an old Stone tradition. But the second name. How about Rebecca? I like the sound of that.'

She shook her head vigorously. 'Sharon!' She signed it letter by letter.

'The Rose of Sharon?' he asked doubtfully. 'Mrs Duggan would cheer to the high heavens, but——'

She smiled at him. Married almost a year, and yet there were still little pockets of things they did not know about each other. It will take all those fifty years ahead to learn everything, she thought.

'Sharon,' she repeated. 'It was my mother's name.'

He leaned over the bed and hugged her, a great bearhug that rattled her frame and tugged at her heart. 'None of that, now,' a passing nurse interrupted. 'Only one person per bed. Hospital rules, you know.'

Mandy pushed him away, giggling. 'I need to tell you something.' He looked at her shining face expectantly. 'In the three hours before Rose was born I was certain she'd be our only child. But twenty-four hours afterwards I know better. We have to have another, Brian. We can't have Rose growing up as an only child.'

'I don't know about that,' he replied grimly. 'In the ten minutes after Rose was born I decided we wouldn't have any more at all. I'm never going to put you through that ordeal again. If more fathers shared delivery-rooms, I suspect there would be a lot fewer babies!'

'Yes, dear,' she signed submissively. 'We'll talk about it later.' He let it pass, not realising that the female of the species had just set the first pinprick in a long campaign to follow.

They held a private party in her bedroom when she arrived home. Mr Rutherford came in, along with Mrs Duggan. Aunt Rose had flown up from Florida, and Brian had libated a bottle of champagne.

'I had to come,' Aunt Rose said. 'I would have flown without the aeroplane, I was that high off the ground. Exciting, you know. Now there are two Rose Stones in the world. It takes a bit of getting used to. I'm proud of you, Amanda.'

'How about me?' Brian complained. 'I could use some congratulations too, you know.'

'Don't let it go to your head,' his aunt returned. 'You were needed at the laying of the keel, but now we're celebrating the launching!'

He put an obviously fake hurt look on his face. His aunt patted him on the arm. 'Of course, dear boy, I congratulate you too. The next one has to be a boy.'

'Now wait a minute, Aunt Rose. Don't start managing my family affairs. I'm fully capable of arranging these little details myself.'

'Yes, of course you are, Brian,' she assured him sweetly as she winked at Mandy. 'Oh, by the way, I saw your friend Meredith in Miami a week ago.'

'No friend of mine,' he laughed. 'She was *your* guest, if I remember correctly. And it was *my* wife who threw her out of our house.'

'Of course I remember,' his aunt purred. 'She was getting a divorce. You know she married that totally unsuitable René François. And now she's hunting again. She expects to come up to Newport for the season.'

'Be we givin' that there charity ball agin in June?' Caleb asked.

'I suppose so,' Brian groaned. 'We've got the only good-sized ballroom in the village. I guess we'll give it, but I won't enjoy it.'

Mandy snapped her fingers. 'I enjoyed the last one so much,' she signed. 'We just have to give another!'

'Don't worry about it,' he returned. '*If* we give one, you're not going!'

'Not going? Of course I'm going.' She spoke carefully, and then reinforced the words by signs. Her fingers crackled with wrath.

'It was great fun, and look what happened to you! I'm not taking any chances. If we give a ball, you, my sweet, are going to be locked up in your bedroom!'

'I'm trying to be polite,' she signed angrily, 'but this is going too far. I——'

He held up his hand and stopped her. 'Wait for the punchline,' he chuckled. 'You're going to be locked up in the bedroom, with me.'

'Oh!' she signed, and then, 'That's not an order, that's an invitation. I accept. Somebody hand me the baby. It's time for her feed.'

Four pairs of hands hastened to share the pleasure. 'Think Miss Clemson might just come to the ball?' Caleb asked. 'I could keep the car handy. Now we've got the hang of it, t'won't be so hard next time.'

'Where did you take that poor girl that night?' Aunt Rose was just making conversation.

'Drove her over to Green Airport,' Caleb allowed. 'She said she wanted a ticket on the first plane out. I got her one.'

Whether it was the wine, the memory of Meredith's departure, or the moment, they all broke out into laughter. Mandy, looking down at the downy head nuzzling her breast, could only find room for thoughts of the man who had brought it all about. *Sweet, biddable Amanda.* Lord, how her father would have roared at that. She could not restrain the giggles. Her entire body shook with a gale of laughter. The shaking was too much for Rose Sharon. The baby squalled with great enthusiasm. Mandy listened proudly to the wonderful sound. *Romantic Amanda Stone,* she told herself, *isn't that the sound of angels singing?*

A look of sheer bliss, of adoration, of—well, to be truthful—worship formed on her face as she looked over the child's head at her husband. Only to find exactly the same look on *his* face as he watched them both, mother and daughter. And silence spoke for love.

Coming Next Month

Available in July wherever paperback books are sold, or through
Harlequin Reader Service:

In the U.S.
P.O. Box 1397
Buffalo, NY
14240-1397

In Canada
P.O. Box 603
Fort Erie, Ontario
L2A 5X3

Summer Reading At Its Best

In July, Harlequin and Silhouette bring readers the Big Summer Read Program. Heat up your summer with these four exciting new novels by top Harlequin and Silhouette authors.

SOMEWHERE IN TIME by Barbara Bretton
YESTERDAY COMES TOMORROW by Rebecca Flanders
A DAY IN APRIL by Mary Lynn Baxter
LOVE CHILD by Patricia Coughlin

From time travel to fame and fortune, this program offers something for everyone.

Available at your favorite retail outlet.

BSR